Parthiban's Dream

Tulika

Parthiban's Dream

abridged and translated by

Nirupama Raghavan

Illustrations by

N. Bindhu Malini

Parthiban's Dream

ISBN 978-81-8146-054-7

First published in India, 2004
Reprinted in 2017

Published by
Tulika Publishers, 24/1 Ganapathy Colony Third Street, Teynampet,
Chennai 600 018, India
email tulikabooks@vsnl.com *website* www.tulikabooks.com

Printed and bound by
Sudarsan Graphics, 27 Neelakanta Mehta Street, T. Nagar,
Chennai 600 017, India

Why I translated Parthiban Kanavu

From the time we moved to Arasavanangkadu near Kumbakonam in Tamil Nadu, and my parents and I began learning Tamil at the same time, I've been able to think in both Tamil and English. When I watch a Tamil movie, I can speak the dialogues in English and vice versa. My parents kind of stopped with the letters of the alphabet and read only the large print. I began enjoying reading in Tamil and went on to read novels and poetry.

When I was 12, my mother caught me translating a poem by Bharatiyar for a friend from Mumbai. So I ended up translating a whole lot of poems.

Two years later, I was coaxed into reading a full-length Tamil novel — *Parthiban Kanavu*. I became interested in the novel somewhere in Book Two, and it was at this time that my mental subtitles began running again. In a fit of absentmindedness I told my mother this, and I was roped, 'kicking and screaming', as the phrase goes, into translating the book.

It was thick. Four hundred and fifty pages of small print? No way! But there I was, poring over the paper. After the first five chapters, I was doing it without any editorial oversight and I finished the translation in ten months. I fell in love with the characters. It was an intriguing and eye-opening experience.

Nirupama Raghavan

Who was Kalki Krishnamurthy?

R. Krishnamurthy was a freedom fighter, social crusader, short story writer, journalist, poet, connoisseur of the arts, novelist and much more. He wrote prolifically in Tamil — over 120 short stories, ten short novels, five novels, three historical romances and hundreds of articles and reviews. He wrote under several pseudonyms, 'Kalki' being one of them.

Kalki was also the name of a magazine he started with a friend in 1941 and his writings became so popular that he began to be known as Kalki Krishnamurthy. In 1943, *Kalki* began serialising his historical novels. The first was *Parthiban Kanavu*. It became a hit and readers waited eagerly for the next instalment and the next, and assiduously cut out the pages from the magazine to bind into a book later. *Parthiban Kanavu* was followed by *Sivakamiyin Sapatham* and then by *Ponniyin Selvan*, the final instalment of which was published in 1951.

At the time, not many people could read because literacy levels were very low. Those who could read were mostly 'English' educated and preferred not to read Tamil. Yet, Kalki's historical novels made such an impact that *Kalki*'s circulation went up to 71,000 copies when the novels were serialised. It was the largest circulation for any weekly in the country during that period. Indeed, it was as much of a phenomenon as Harry Potter is today.

What was so special about his historical novels? Well, it was the first time that a writer was using ancient South Indian history as background for fiction. For another, he used simple yet evocative language, drawing his strength from the force and effectiveness of everyday speech. This was instantly appealing. Then, his characters were so alive, his plots so fast paced that readers began to identify themselves with the period and the people. History, without their knowledge, walked right into their homes.

Some believe he was a 'populist' writer, but there is no doubt he was a progressive one. He wrote about many unfortunate practices that were rampant at the time — and persist to this day — such as untouchability and the oppression of women. He won the Sahitya Akademi award in 1956, two years after his death, for *Alai Osai*, serialised in *Kalki* in 1948-49 and published as a book in 1963.

Kalki's birth centenary was celebrated on 9 September 1999. This translation, done over a hundred years after his birth, by a 15-year-old who spontaneously responded to the joie de vivre of *Parthiban Kanavu*, is testimony to its universal appeal.

BOOK ONE

At the Ferry Dock

The banks of the Kaveri were calm. The rising sun's red-gold rays touched the waters so they shimmered brightly. The river's other name, Ponni, the golden one, described it well. The morning breeze played gently, forming eddies and small whirlpools in the swift waters. Waves lapped against each other and the flying foam sparkled like bright jewels. The Kaveri was a magical sight.

On the northeast side of this expanse of water was a lush, tree-filled island, and on the island towered a majestic palace. Its golden dome glittered brilliantly.

The early morning sounds set off the silence of the river. The birds in the banyan trees draped all along the river made loud conversation in welcome of the dawn. They ruffled their feathers and left to search for food. A lone peepal tree swayed as if to reaffirm its existence. The river pushed and pulled at the ferries tied to the aerial roots of the banyans, muttering sullenly to itself when it did not succeed.

Under a banyan tree some distance from the riverbank stood a hut from which came the tantalising scent of kambu adai, maize pancakes. A buffalo lay peacefully tied to a stake beside the hut, calmly chewing cud.

Inside, a young woman was cooking. A young man sat nearby,

eating with relish. "I don't know if I will have the opportunity of eating your kambu adai and keerai kozhambu again, Valli!" he said, smacking his lips.

"You've been saying this every morning for the last month," she replied sharply, "And I don't want to hear it any more!"

"I'm not joking, Valli. I will fall at the king's feet and ask him to take me with him when the war comes."

"Then I shall fall at your feet and ask you to take me with you. If you don't, then take me to the middle of the Kaveri and drown me!"

"A woman go to war while the men hide at home? What next!" said the young man. "Wait! Are those hoofbeats?" His voice trembled with excitement. Leaving the food where it was, he ran to the doorway.

A warrior who had just dismounted from his horse called out, "Ponna! I have urgent news for the king. Take out the boat quickly!"

"Valli!" said Ponnan. "There's news from Uraiyur. The message seems to be urgent. I'll be back."

"Fine. It's an urgent message, so you're going to leave with your stomach half-full. This is too much!" exclaimed Valli and turned away her face.

"What do you expect, Valli? It is royal work after all," said Ponnan, coming close to her. He gently turned her towards him. Just then the soldier called out again. Ponnan jumped as if shaken from a trance, and quickly left the house.

The Royal Family

Valli's mind wandered restlessly as she did her housework after Ponnan left. She felt some momentous event was about to occur and she peeped out of the door every now and then.

In a little while, a group of ten or fifteen cavalrymen arrived at the docks from the direction of the capital, Uraiyur. In the middle of the group were two riderless white stallions and an ivory palanquin carried by eight burly men. They set the palanquin down at the docks, the cavalrymen dismounted and tied their horses to the trees. One of the horsemen, Velappan, saw Valli and came up to chat with her.

Valli asked him why the king was leaving the island — Vasanta Maaligai, Island of Spring — so early. He replied, "For the last four or five years, our king has not paid taxes to the Pallava emperor, Chakravarti Narasimha Varman. The emperor has now returned from his wars in the north. It seems he is sending messengers today to enquire why our king has not paid taxes. The king will refuse to pay and there will undoubtedly be a war."

"Why do we have to fight a war for this? Wouldn't it be simpler to pay all four years' taxes at one go and forget the whole business?" asked Valli innocently.

"The king will not do that. He says a decision once taken must not be reversed."

While Valli and Velappan were talking to each other, they saw the royal ferry making its way to the shore from the summer palace.

King Parthiban, Queen Arulmozhi Devi, and their son, Vikraman, were seated in it. Two burly guards with swords at their hips and tridents in their hands stood on either side. Ponnan and another man were rowing the ferry. As soon as it docked, the two guards leapt out and cried, "All hail the King of kings, lord of the Chola realm, the ever victorious King Parthiban!" The soldiers standing on the shore cried out: "Victory to the king!" Velappan had already rejoined the soldiers.

When the king alighted from the ferry, he came towards the hut and beckoned to Valli who was standing in the doorway. She quickly ran to him and bent down to touch his feet.

"Valli! Does Ponnan take good care of you?" asked the king. Valli bowed her head and smiled.

"Ask if she takes good care of Ponnan," said the queen slyly, "and she will answer you quickly."

The king laughed and said, "Valli! Did you hear what the maharani said? Take good care of Ponnan or some day he will rescue someone else from a flood as he once rescued you."

But Ponnan was not listening to the banter. He said, "Maharaja! I have a boon to ask of you. When the armies leave for the battlefield, I beg that this humble servant be allowed to accompany them."

The king was silent for a while. Then he said, "Ponna! I can see what you are thinking. I know why you ask to come with us to war. But tell me, if I do not return from the battlefield, whom else could I trust to teach the prince to swim?" Ponnan and Valli's eyes instantly filled with tears.

When the royals and their escort had left and gone some distance, Valli became her old self again. Turning to Ponnan she said, "Did you hear what the maharaja said? You must not do anything without my permission."

"Well, in that case," said Ponnan, "I shall set out immediately. Valli, I have to go to Uraiyur this afternoon. The messengers sent to ask for taxes are arriving today. The maharaja is going to refuse them. I must be there. I must!"

Valli folded her hands together in front of her and said, mimicking Ponnan's voice, "Maharaja, I have a boon to ask of you. When your armies leave for the battlefield, may this humble servant accompany them?"

"Oh, shut up! If you're going to keep teasing me about this, I won't go!" said Ponnan irritatedly and went off in a sulk to sit by the river.

A little while later, they heard the sound of horses' hooves. Five horses went by. They were heading towards Uraiyur at a furious pace. The leader held a banner upon which was painted a lion.

Valli and Ponnan silently watched them go. "Which flag was that?" asked Valli finally.

"Pallava," replied Ponnan. "I have to get to Uraiyur before they leave. If you come along, you can also visit your grandfather."

The Pallava Messengers

Uraiyur was one kada away from the dock. Fourteen hundred years ago, this was a considerable distance. At the time, royalty used horses, elephants or chariots; commoners travelled by cart or on foot. Huge highways or rajapattais used to be cleared from city to city for easy travel and transportation.

During Parthiban's time, the Chola lands were a fraction of what they had once been. On one side, the Pandiyans threatened them and on the other, the Pallavas were rising swiftly. Between these two, they had penned in the Cholas securely. But the Kaveri kept the kingdom lush.

The road Ponnan and Valli travelled by was edged on one side by the furious flow of the Kaveri. On the other side lay verdant fields bordered by gracious palms and waving thickets of sugarcane and banana. The land, right up to the horizon, was a carpet of green. Water gurgled gleefully through the irrigation canals, and white cranes fished in them.

This was the peaceful, fertile country that would soon be shattered by war.

By the time Valli and Ponnan reached the fortress of Uraiyur, the shadows were lengthening. The sun had lost its footing and had slipped beneath the horizon. When they neared the outer gates, the inner gates crashed open and a small group of horsemen trotted out. The leader held a Lion flag in his hands. Valli and Ponnan knew immediately that these were the soldiers who had ridden past their home that afternoon. The Pallava messengers were returning. Instinctively, they flattened themselves against the walls. As the horses crossed the outer gates, they sprang into a gallop and took off as fast as the wind. Ponnan and Valli watched the dust swirling behind them until they vanished into the dusk and distance.

The rambling streets of Uraiyur were filled with clusters of people speaking to each other excitedly. Ponnan and Valli joined one of the groups. "Ah! How shall I find words to describe the sight!" said one man. "The king sat upon his throne. You could have heard a pin drop anywhere in the palace. Then he said, 'Send the messengers in!' What vigour, what majesty in his voice! The envoy entered the room. Their leader came to the front and saluted the king. 'What message do you bring?' asked the king. The man replied, 'We are the emissaries of the emperor of Kanchi. Since the time of your grandfather, we have collected tribute from your kingdom. You have paid no taxes now for six years. The chakravarti has sent me to enquire why.' "

"Ah! If only I could describe how the king looked then!" said another. "When he said, 'O messenger! Tell your emperor that I shall deliver the tribute in the battlefield!' my hair stood on end. The emissary was taken aback. He said after a pause, 'Then I have been instructed to say that His Majesty wishes you to prepare for war. The Pallava regiments will have already left Kanchi while I speak to you. His Majesty says that the Chola king shall decide the place and day of battle and inform him.' To this, our king replied, 'The day of the full moon of the month of

Purattasi, upon the banks of the river Vennar, we shall stand ready.' When they heard this, the people in the court all shouted 'Viravel! Vettrivel!' "

Ponnan and Valli followed the roads further into town. By this time, night had fallen. The moon shone dully through huge banks of soft, grey-white clouds. Lamps were being lit at street corners and the wicks sent slim spirals of smoke towards the sky. And then, from some high tower, a reverberating drumbeat thundered into the night. Then another. And another. Dhammmmmm. Dhammmmmmm. Dhammmmmmm. Dhammmmmmm. From every high place, the drums that were struck on festivals and royal celebrations were being crashed by unseen hands. Tonight it was a summons to fight. Single beats, evenly spaced, went out in every direction from every tower and tall building in Uraiyur. The echoes rang through the squares and streets. Adhammmm. Adhammmmm. The echoes overlapped and slammed into the ears of all those who heard it. After a few moments, the sound of the drums that piled over each other from the various towers seemed to be saying: Yuddham. Yuddham. Yuddham. War. War. War.

"The summons has gone out," said Ponnan. His voice sounded so strange that Valli was startled.

"What has happened to you?" she cried.

"Nothing!" said Ponnan sharply. "Nothing is wrong with me!" After a short pause he said, "I shall go to the war, Valli. I must!"

Grandfather and Granddaughter

Ponnan and Valli went to her grandfather's house on Kammal Street, where all the blacksmiths lived. Her grandfather and grandmother were very happy to see them. Ponnan paid his respects and left as quickly as he could, saying he had an appointment with the king. Valli talked excitedly with her grandfather. Suddenly she cried out, "Oh my God! What is that?" Stacked in a corner of the veranda were several daggers, swords and spears.

"What indeed?" said her grandfather. "Swords and spears and tridents, of course, thirsting to chop Pallava heads like fruit! Not that you would have seen any of those. Why, in the old days . . ."

"Don't frighten me!" said Valli, alarmed.

"Very soon even the men in the land will be as cowardly as you! Do you know, during the times of my grandfather and great-grandfather, the forges were lit day and night. Sharp swords and spears were made, and tridents gleamed in the sun. All the smithies were alive and bustling. But those golden days began to set even during my father's time. In all my considerable days, this is the first time I have made swords and spears — or even seen them. Oh, why did this war not come twenty years ago!"

"Oh God! And here I was hoping that you would convince my husband that he should not go to the war!"

"Ponnan? Go to the war? Nonsense!"

"He goes on and on about going to the war."

"You are the last of your line," said her grandfather. "He will not be allowed to go. The last of a line is always exempted from battle."

There was a tragic reason behind her grandfather's words. Virabhadra Achari's family had once been large and bustling. Four years ago, everyone in the family save Valli's grandparents had gone to a wedding on the other side of the river. There was a flash flood and the small boat carrying them across had capsized. Ponnan, who had been standing on the shore, had jumped in and tried to save those he could from drowning. But only Valli had survived, as though by some divine grace. Everyone else had drowned.

"But why is the war taking place at all?" said Valli. "I do not understand. It seems so unnecessary."

"Why the war? Why? Have you heard of honour? That is why this war! How can the Tiger bow down to the Bull? How can the Chola nation bow down to the Pallavas? This dishonour is what this war tries to erase," said her grandfather.

"I saw the flag this afternoon," said Valli. "It had a lion, not a bull."

"Yes, they have changed the bull to a lion," said her grandfather. "Twenty years ago, Mahendra Chakravarti was the ruler in Kanchi. Tales of his valour were being told all over the country. At that time, Pulikesi, the Chalukya king of Vatapi in the north, invaded the Pallava kingdom with a huge force. The chakravarti realised that he would not stand a chance if he tried open warfare. So he and all his people shut themselves up in Kanchi. When Pulikesi realised that it was useless laying siege to Kanchi, he marched further south to the northern shore of the Kollidam. Our Parthiban had just begun to rule and he set about gathering troops. What a mess Uraiyur was in! But by then, Pulikesi had some trouble on his borders to the north and he had to retreat. He did not cross the Kollidam. But the atrocities he unleashed upon the land that he crossed were unspeakable. Whole towns were destroyed, razed to the ground. With that, Mahendra Varman's reputation dimmed. He did not live long after that and Narasimha Varman became emperor. His sole ambition was to avenge the defeat at the hands of the Chalukyas. He assembled a formidable army. Finally, six years ago, he went north with the army. He killed Pulikesi on the battlefield and burnt Vatapi to the ground. To commemorate the event, he changed the emblem of the Pallavas from the bull to the lion. It is but a month since he returned." The old man's voice trailed away.

Valli, who had been listening intently all this while, said, "Why does our king wish to fight this man? He should be a friend to him!"

A horse that came galloping down the road stopped at the door, directly beneath them. "Virabhadra Achari!" rang out an authoritative voice.

Immediately Valli's grandfather said, "It's that Marappa Bhupathi. Go inside, quick, or he might see you."

Marappa Bhupathi

Marappa Bhupathi was a hefty fellow in his mid-twenties. He was dressed like royalty. Restlessness and frustration were etched on his features. "The Crown Prince is welcome in my house," said the old man courteously.

"Crown Prince? Crown Prince who? That little *!*!* who was born yesterday is the Crown Prince. Jaya vijayi bhava!" he cried mockingly. After a pause, he said, "Tell me, what do your seashells reveal, Achari?"

Other than being a blacksmith, Virabhadra Achari also was a master astrologer. "I have consulted my shells. Tell me what you wish to know, and I shall do my best," he said.

"The war, obviously. How shall it end? If you cannot tell me even this, I shall personally take the palm scrolls you consult and the seashells you study and throw them into the Kaveri!" exclaimed Marappa Bhupathi.

"Do that," said the old man agreeably. "I don't need them, they are of no use to me. I have only one girl to continue my lineage."

"How's Valli?" asked Marappa Bhupathi. His face took on an odd expression.

"She's alive," replied the old man curtly.

"If Ponnan goes to the war and does not return, what will Valli do?" asked Marappa Bhupathi slyly.

"God and I will take care of her!" replied the old man fiercely.

"But we digress. What will be the result of this war?"

"One side shall lose all its men but I do not know which."

"For this, I need neither you nor your shells. The Chola army will be annihilated. What an honour Parthiban will earn!"

"Prince, this is not the way to speak! Whatever differences you and the king have, while you face a common enemy . . ."

"Who is our enemy? The greatest enemy of the Chola nation is Parthiban. The Pallava army is huge. Their land stretches from the Kaveri to the Godavari. Narasimha Pallavar is a formidable warrior. He travelled all the way to Vatapi, killed Pulikesi, burnt his city, and returned. We declare war on him? Parthiban's brave act is like a mosquito declaring war on an elephant!" exclaimed Marappa Bhupathi.

"Why tell me?" said the old man. "Tell the king!"

"Do you think I haven't? The result was that I lost my post of General! The king has appointed himself General. He says he will lead the troops to war. Let him! Who wants to be General anyway?"

"Then you won't go to war?"

"If the king calls me, I shall go. If not, no!" said Marappa

Bhupathi. “And if I go to war, I shall return dead, as a ghost, and possess Valli!” he added and laughed. Then he stood up and spotted the weapons lying on the ground. “Ah! Very sharp weapons indeed! Knives! Swords! Spears! Garden implements! And he talks of winning! What a joke!” he said as he went out of the house.

The anger in the old man’s eyes was as bright as a spark of fire from his forge.

Omens of War

When she heard the horse leave, Valli emerged, eyes glittering with fury. "What use is it making all these knives and armour? You let a man insult our king and walk away!"

"You said we shouldn't fight."

"All I said was that I didn't understand why the war was taking place!" said Valli, her eyes brimming with tears.

"Yes, Valli! That rascal interrupted me. When Narasimha Pallavar set out on his campaign, he sent a message to our king, asking for his help. Parthiban replied that he would help, on condition that Uraiyur would no longer pay taxes to the Pallava empire. Narasimha Pallavar simply gathered his troops and left. And our king stopped paying taxes. Now tell me. Is our king right, or should he surrender to the emperor?"

"Yes, I think I do see that our king is right," said Valli thoughtfully. Then with sudden fierceness, she added, "And all those people who speak against him should go to hell! Do you know how good our king is?"

Her grandfather became fierce in his turn. "Yes, I do. He is a good man. And that is precisely why he takes this mannerless rogue whose family has rotted to pieces, and indulges him!"

"What are you saying, Thatha?"

"I know exactly what I am saying. This Marappa Bhupathi is not even a true brother of the king. The earlier king married some old shrew in his old age. Nobody liked it. That nag's son is this Marappa Bhupathi. He was the Crown Prince until Vikraman was born. And I have to put up with him because of you."

"WHAT?"

"Be very careful around him, Valli. He will not go to the war. He once wanted your hand in marriage by consent or force. I knew from the stars that some great catastrophe was to befall our family. I did not want my family murdered resisting his men and so I sent you all across the river. But death came anyway.

After you had left by boat, the man arrived with a troop of soldiers, just as I thought. To pacify him, I told him that he was fated to be the son-in-law of a great emperor. Ever since, he's been plaguing me," said her grandfather.

"Now I see what he meant when he spoke about me. You will have to protect me if my husband goes to war, Thatha!" Valli said and gripped both his hands tightly.

"Idiot! Of course your husband will not go! The king has forbidden him," said Virabhadra Achari.

Just then, there was a loud clash of drums outside and a crier announced, "Vettrivel! Viravel! War comes! War comes! For the honour of the Chola nation! War comes! Men who are lame, blind, simple or the only son are exempted. All others may enlist! Viravel! Vettrivel!!" And the drums rolled again, deafeningly.

Virabhadra Achari and Valli stepped into the street. Far away in the sky, to the south, a star suddenly gleamed with a bright, final glory. Then it hurtled down the sky and winked out. When she saw it, Valli shivered.

At exactly the same time, Ponnan too saw the star. He too shivered. He was walking down the road to the palace. There were four days to the full moon. Uraiyur's many-storeyed houses shone white and glowed in the silver light. It was ethereal.

In those days, Uraiyur was the capital and Tiruchirapalli, or Chirapalli as it was called then, was a small village. Now, Uraiyur is but a village and Tiruchirapalli a bustling city.

Anyhow, the king and the prince had been on the Chirapalli hill a short while ago — Virabhadra Achari had told Ponnan that. He also knew why they had gone there. It was upon that hill that the disgrace of the Chola nation had been marked out most clearly. There, etched upon the walls, was a full-length carving of Parthiban's father kneeling submissively in front of Chakravarti Mahendra Varman. *How much longer shall we be forced to accept this dishonour*, thought Ponnan. *When shall we erase this stain?* And now, when the chance had come to do something about it, he had been forbidden from fighting. Thinking about all these things, Ponnan continued to walk swiftly down the road.

Arulmozhi Devi

Arulmozhi Devi was seated on a marble bench in a corner of the garden filled with the scent of shenbaga — magnolia — flowers. Her personal couriers had reported back to her the minute the king's audience with the Pallava messengers had ended.

The almost-full moon shone serenely in the sky. Memories flooded Arulmozhi Devi. She had married Parthiban twelve years ago and had lived here since. They had talked so often sitting on this bench, scarcely aware of the passage of time. And when Vikraman was born, she and the king had sat here and played with the baby prince.

But all the while, a secret sorrow had gnawed at Parthiban's heart, like a festering wound. Arulmozhi discovered what this was only after their marriage, and the fact that she was partly the cause of the sorrow greatly distressed her.

Arulmozhi was the daughter of a minor Chera king. After Arulmozhi's marriage to Parthiban had been finalised, Pallava messengers had arrived to ask for her hand for their Crown Prince. Her parents had been willing to go back on their word but Arulmozhi had flatly rejected the offer, saying she had chosen Parthiban. Mahendra Chakravarti had then withdrawn his proposal and Crown Prince Narasimha Pallavar had married a Pandiyan princess. Parthiban had come to know of this much after their marriage and he constantly worried that Arulmozhi regretted marrying him when she could have been an empress. After Vikraman was born, the worries increased and Parthiban said several times that the only name he could pass on to his son was that of being a brave father.

Now the time had come to prove that statement. She had thought that at least she could die with him as wives did in the old days, but Parthiban would not allow that. She had to stay alive for her son's sake, he had said. But how could she even think of living without him? As she sat thinking about this, she began to sob.

"Arulmozhi, I thought you were a courageous wife! This is not the time to be a coward!" came Parthiban's stern voice from behind her. She whirled around. "Come. Let us go to the palace." They went towards the palace, holding hands but not saying a word . . . all of them had already been said, sometime or the other. When they went in, the arati was going on in the temple, the day's devotions were drawing to an end.

After the priest had left, the king lifted a box from the feet of the Vishnu idol. He said, "Devi, you always wanted to know what was in this box. It is now time for me to tell you."

He opened the box. Inside were a sword and a manuscript. The sword's handle shone brightly with gold and jewels. The blade was polished and keen. In contrast, the manuscript looked old and unassuming.

"The manuscript is the Tirukkural, as written by Tiruvalluvar himself. This blade was the sword of my ancestors, Karikal Valavan and Nedumudikkilli," said Parthiban reverently. "I have never used it, for I felt that a vassal should not wield the sword of an emperor. These two things are the heirlooms of the Chola dynasty. It is your duty to safeguard them, and when Vikraman is of age, you shall pass them on to him. Tell him this: When he is a free ruler of even a small patch of land, and rules as the Tirukkural dictates he must, only then shall he wear this sword. Swear to me, here, that you shall fulfil this task."

When Arulmozhi heard this, her eyes filled with tears. "As you command, my king," she said in a choked voice.

"And may God give you the courage to do so," he said as he stroked her hair and wiped the tears on her face.

The Palace of Arts

The Chitthira Mandapam or Palace of Arts on the west side of Uraiyur was famous throughout the southern part of the subcontinent. Even the gallery at Kanchi, which was built up by Mahendra Chakravarti, was said to be not a patch on it. Parthiban and Vikraman came riding down the royal road on identical white horses and as they reached the entrance to the Chitthira Mandapam and alighted from their horses, they met Ponnan.

"Ponna! What are you doing here?" asked the king. Ponnan's silence helped him gauge his state of mind. "Here, Ponna, take the torch!" said the king. Ponnan took a burning torch from the guard and followed them into the Palace of Arts, holding up the light so they could see. They went to a door that was always kept locked and guarded.

The king opened the door and said, "Go in, Ponna, and hold the torch high. Do not take it close to the wall or the paintings will be blackened and spoilt." There were pictures on the wall, just like there were all over the palace. The torchlight flickered in the shadowy room as the king stepped in behind Ponnan, leading Vikraman by the hand.

"My son," said the king, "You have asked me many times

what I have kept locked up in this room. Now is the time to tell you. Vikrama! No one, not even your mother, has been here. I have deliberately kept this room dark and unknown, the drawings unseen. Ponna! Hold the torch higher!"

"Do you see that drawing?" he continued. "The first one? Tell me what you see."

"A country's forces leaving for war," replied the prince. "Oh! Look at the size of the army! Elephants and horses and soldiers! There are so many of them!" exclaimed Vikraman with awe. Then he whirled around abruptly and gazed at his father's face intently. "Father!" he said, and his voice trailed away hesitantly. "Did you draw these?"

"Yes, I did. These last twelve years, night and day, asleep or awake, these are the dreams that I have seen. And this is where I have drawn them. Do you see whose forces these are?"

"Yes, I do! The Tiger flag flies at the head of the army. These are Chola forces, aren't they? But father, where is the king?"

"Vikrama!" said the king softly. "I have deliberately left the elephant riderless. The day a child of the Chola line gathers an army and leaves his land for a campaign, having established his nation, only on that day shall the rider be drawn upon these walls. Today, the Cholas are insignificant vassals. Hemmed in by the Cheras, the Pandiyas and the Pallavas, we have diminished to a fist-sized land." Parthiban's voice was choked with sorrow.

"But it was not always so," he continued. "Our ancestors were renowned emperors. Among them Karikal Valavan and Nedumudikkilli stand tall, warriors and kings beyond compare. In those days, the Pallavas were virtually non-existent, and the Pandiyas and the Cheras were our vassals. Kings from faraway lands beyond the sea would send tribute to the Chola chakravarti. Ships left from Kaveripattinam for foreign shores, returning with precious jewels and great treasures to fill the coffers of the Chola Empire. To return this glory to the country that I love so much — that is the desire which fills my heart to overflowing. This is the dream I see, night and day, asleep, awake . . . always it fills my eyes."

"There! Do you see that painting, the one on the other side?" the king said as he and Vikraman walked from painting to painting. The Cholas were depicted crossing a mighty river, climbing a high mountain. Vast forces stood opposed to them. The triumphant Cholas were shown receiving tributes and gifts from defeated kings. The Chola army reached the Himalayas, and the Tiger flag flew victoriously from the white mountains. The last scenes showed the troops returning to their homeland, being welcomed by the joyous people. On the other sides, exquisitely portrayed, were proud ships setting sail, flying the flag of the Chola Empire.

Vikraman's Oath

When Vikraman had finished looking at all the paintings, he returned to his father's side and said, "Father?"

The King turned to him and said, his voice filled with love, "Ask, my son. Whatever you wish to know, ask today. It may be your last chance."

"Father! These paintings are beautiful! Who taught you to draw like this? Even the paintings in the Chitthira Mandapam are not as beautiful as this!" The king swept his son into his arms and embraced him tightly.

"But Father, why did you never reveal this to anyone else? Surely you could not have been ashamed of such marvellous paintings! How real the figures are! How filled with life! Why have you not exposed these to the people of our country? How could you deny them the love and awe that these paintings inspire?" said Vikraman forcefully.

His father replied quietly, but just as forcefully. "In this world, wealth and power are sometimes prized over true talent. Mahendra Chakravarti ruled in Kanchi. A sabha of learned men conferred upon him the title 'King of artists'. The present chakravarti has many titles. The Narada of music! The Vishwakarma of sculptors! This is how the world describes him. Why? Because he has a vast army, he is the emperor of a huge kingdom.

"Son, God doesn't care about rich or poor. A cobbler is the same as a chakravarti to him. But those who represent him in this world sometimes believe that God is behind every powerful or wealthy person. Mahendran was a Jain for a while, did you know that? Then, one fine morning, he woke up and said he had realised the truth. He pretended to be a devotee of Shiva!

"Mahendra and Narasimha Pallavar are both masters of disguise. They have fooled the entire world into believing their devotion to the Hindu gods. Only the Cholas are interested in preserving the worship of Vishnu and Shiva in the land. Yet Shivanadiyars and Vaishnava elders frequent the court of the emperor of Kanchi.

"Do you see now why I do not want my drawings to be displayed?" Parthiban continued saying to his son. "People will sneer at me. 'So Parthiban the petty vassal has taken up drawing too, has he?' they will say. And you have not taken another factor into account..."

"What is that?" asked Vikraman, puzzled.

"These are not just paintings scribbled on a wall, Vikrama! These are my deepest dreams, my most heartfelt desires and aspirations. Were someone to see these today, they would scorn me as a fool who daydreams but can never fulfil his idle wishes. That is why I have left this hall unknown and dark. When these dreams start becoming realities, then let light enter within these walls, let people glimpse what lies inside and rejoice. That dream will not be fulfilled in my time. I hope that at least in your lifetime my dream comes true. Now, my son, now do you realise why I refused to let you come to the battlefield with me?"

"Yes, Father, I understand now."

"You must live, not die, for your country. And, living, try to make my dream a reality. The good of this country shall be your life. The glory of the Chola lineage shall be your only thought. Your only concern shall be the Chola flag flying higher than any other flag. I am leaving Uraiyur the day after tomorrow. I may not return. The Puranas say that those who die fighting go to heaven. But I shall never go to that heaven. My heart lies within this land, and here I shall return. This country is my heaven. In the lush fields, in the temple ponds, on the banks of the Kaveri, and within the coconut groves, my spirit shall dwell after my death. And, while I reside there unknown, perhaps if someone were to say, 'Vikraman, son of Parthiban, brought fame and wealth to the Chola people,' there would be no greater joy. This is all I desire of you. Will you do this for me?"

"I will, Father. I swear I will," said Vikraman, tears streaming down his cheeks.

Ponnan, who had been listening soundlessly, found that his eyes too had filled with tears, and his cheeks were wet. The king turned to him and said, "You have been listening, haven't you? Don't you think that someone who truly loves the prince must stay with him? That is why I have forbidden you to fight. It would be a greater help to me were you to stay with the prince and protect him. Will you stay?"

Ponnan replied in a trembling voice, "I shall stay, my king."

The Troops Depart

Uraiyur had never been in such a bustle. Though it was still dawn, everyone was outdoors, awaiting the soldiers' departure. The drums were beating again, it was the final call to war. Spears slamming against each other, farewells being called from mothers and lovers, horses neighing impatiently.

Every man reported to the palace in time. The higher-ranking officers quickly split the new recruits into groups and divisions — cavalry, elephant drivers and foot soldiers — all flying the Chola flag at the head of the company. The musicians joined them with conches and drums. Shouts of "Viravel! Vettrivel! Viravel! Vettrivel!" rent the air.

A cry went up from behind the still-shut palace gates: "The king is coming!" To roars of "Jaya vijayi bhava! Victory to the king!" The king himself emerged from the palace. He wore yellow garments beneath battle armour. He also wore his sword. The queen and the prince followed close behind. When they reached the gates, the queen placed a garland of lilies about his neck and did an arati for him. Then she dipped her finger in turmeric water and made a mark upon his forehead. Again there were cries of "Viravel! Vettrivel! Jaya vijayi bhava!" The king stood, measuring the crowd with his eyes, scanning and searching.

A messenger came up to him. When the king had given him permission to speak, the messenger said, "Your Majesty, Marappa Bhupathi was setting out with the army, but he fell down and is unconscious. We took him to the palace, but he has not yet recovered."

The corners of the king's mouth twitched. He said to the messenger, "You may go. Tell Bhupathi when he recovers that I told him to guard his delicate constitution well." Then the king turned to Vikraman, who was standing on the other side, and swept him up in a brief, fierce embrace, burying his face in his son's hair. "Remember what I told you, son. You will not forget it, will you?" he said.

Vikraman said, "No, Father. I shall never forget."

The king took his son's hand and gave it to his wife, saying,

"Devi! Bid me farewell with a smile." Queen Arulmozhi, her eyes filling with tears, throat choked with emotion, replied, "By God's grace, your dream shall come true. Go, and return safely." Her chest felt tight with sorrow.

The king climbed upon his elephant. Again the drums rolled, the cymbals clashed, the conches blew. And then, all at once, not a step out of place, not a man looking back, the army of the Cholas set off to meet their fate.

The Battlefield

The full moon of the month of Purattasi shone upon the banks of the river Vennar, illuminating a gory sight. The moon ducked behind the grey clouds, emerging, it seemed, reluctantly. All day long a ferocious battle had raged, and now the blood of the dead ran in the river, making the waters purple-red. The west bank was littered with bodies. The shadows of vultures filled the field. The murmur of the river was deceptively soothing. In that terrifying tableau of silver moon and screaming birds, shadows and blood, a solitary figure walked swiftly and silently.

On closer observation, it could be seen that the figure was that of a Shivanadiyar, a devotee of Lord Shiva. He had long, matted hair, a forehead liberally smeared with ash, a beard traced with grey, a string of rudraksha beads around his neck. He wore saffron robes and a tiger-skin. He held a kamandalam, a water pot, in his hand. A piercing gaze, keen and quick, glowing with calm intelligence, flashed from unusually large eyes. He was well built but lean. His stride was measured, confident, assured and noble.

Suddenly he stopped. The royal elephant of the Cholas had risen, swaying, to its feet. The elephant was mortally wounded, yet it staggered forward, careful not to step on the dead. It was searching for someone. It then reached a large pile of bodies and stopped. It lifted the bodies off the pile one by one, gently.

The Shivanadiyar stepped closer, hid behind a lone tree, and watched. The elephant found the man it was looking for at the very bottom of the pile. It stroked his face a few times. There was no reaction from the man. The elephant moved away from him and raised its trunk towards the sky. A cry of sorrow and suffering emanated from its throat. The sound rose like a ghost

and went beyond the battlefield, over the river, past the fields, and seemed to rip apart the very fabric of the sky, echoing and echoing, and then disappearing into the night. Then, as if unable to bear the pain any longer, the great elephant shuddered and fell to the ground, like a mountain shivering through an earthquake. Then – nothing! The silence of the battlefield returned.

The Shivanadiyar crossed over and peered at the man whom the elephant had been looking for. It was King Parthiban. He knelt down and touched the fallen king's forehead and chest. Then he carefully placed the king's head in his lap and sprinkled water from his kamandalam on his face. The king slowly regained consciousness. With eyes half-open and glazed, he gazed at the man bending over him and asked faintly, "My good sir, who are you?"

The Shivanadiyar replied, "I am the follower of the followers of Shiva. I heard of your bravery upon the battlefield today. I came because I wanted to meet such a man as you. Your valour and courage shall never dim."

"How did the war end?" asked Parthiban, making a great effort to speak. Both dread and eagerness were reflected in his dull eyes.

"Is there any doubt about that? Can't you hear the Pallavas rejoicing in their camp?"

Parthiban's face crumpled. "But did any of the Chola troops…" he asked.

"No, Parthiba. Not one survived. They fought until the last man was killed."

Parthiban's eyes filled with relief and satisfaction. "There is hope yet," he whispered. "You have given me great happiness in my dying moments. How can I return this grace?"

"I do not need a reward. My life's work is to serve the brave. If you have any sorrow, any unfulfilled desire, tell me. I shall do my best to redeem it," said the Shivanadiyar.

"Truly? Then I am lucky indeed. Yes, I have one sorrow in my heart. My country has lost its glory and pride, it lies in ruins. I dreamt of the Tiger flag flying on faraway shores but this remained a dream during my lifetime. In my son's time, at least, my dream must come true. This is my wish. My son must become a valorous man. Not life, not comfort, but honour, freedom and courage must be his ideals. He must learn to hate being a king who bows to a foreigner. This is my wish. Will you fulfil it, my lord?"

Parthiban's pain-wracked body was strained by his efforts to speak and he fell back weakly, still watching the Shivanadiyar.

The Shivanadiyar said softly, "Parthiba! I shall satisfy your desire, if I live to complete it."

"Then I am truly blessed. I have nothing to keep me from death. But – but – who are you? Lord Shiva, whom I prayed to night and day?"

"No, Parthiba! Do not call me a god." After a second's pause, he continued, "I, too, am a mortal, touched by death. Do you want to know who I am? Very well, then look!" And he ripped off the long hair and beard. They came away easily in his hand.

When Parthiban saw the face revealed to him in the moonlight, his darkening eyes opened wide. "Sir, it is you?" he asked, in a stunned voice. Depthless amazement and awe shone in his eyes. Then his eyes closed and Parthiban's tired spirit fled from the body that had held it so long.

BOOK TWO

The Shivanadiyar

It was half an hour before dawn. Venus had risen ahead of the sun. The Kaveri's headlong rush towards its final destination was the only sound. Suddenly, there came the clatter of horse-hooves on the road from Srirangam to Uraiyur.

It was a large, high-bred stallion carrying a tall, well-built warrior. His face was in shadow and he bore no outward sign of rank or identity. The horse had evidently run for a long time and was now being walked so that it could recoup its energy.

The Kaveri, secure in her beauty and strength, flowed quietly on his right. The left was a tangled mass of foliage. The man wheeled the horse sharply into this mass. It pushed through familiarly to a narrow trail overhung with creepers and bushes, but rider and horse knew where to go. Presently they came to a clearing in which stood an Ayyanar temple, with its many terracotta statues, both old and new.

The man entered the clearing and got off the horse. He then opened the saddlebag and hastily pulled out some things. In seconds, the warrior had disappeared and was replaced by the saintly form of the Shivanadiyar. He stuffed the warrior clothes, ornaments and weapons back into the bag and hid it behind a stone elephant. He patted the horse's neck affectionately.

The horse whinnied softly, acknowledging the gesture. Then the man walked back the way he had come.

After half an hour, he stopped in front of Ponnan's hut and called out. Ponnan rushed out and fell at the Shivanadiyar's feet, Valli right behind him. Then they all went inside, where the Shivanadiyar sat on a mat that had been spread out for him. In a while, Ponnan left to fetch the queen and the prince, leaving Valli with the Shivanadiyar.

Valli's Gossip

Valli made hot kambu adais for the Shivanadiyar. Between mouthfuls he asked her, "How is the queen these days?"

"She appears brave when the prince is near, but collapses when he goes away," said Valli. "If any mishap befalls the prince, the queen will die."

"Do you know if the people support him?"

"The people are solidly behind the prince and against the Pallavas. My husband and I must have talked to hundreds of thousands of people by now."

"And how is that Marappa Bhupathi? Does he still come for predictions to your grandfather?"

"He still comes, the fool," said Valli. Then she burst into uncontrollable giggles.

"What do you find amusing, good lady?" asked the Shivanadiyar.

"Do you know what Marappa Bhupathi's pet dream is? He wants to marry the daughter of the Kanchi emperor, Kuntavi herself!"

For an instant, the Shivanadiyar's face darkened with anger. Then he smiled. "So?" he asked.

"Where is the chakravarti's daughter, and where this fool?

There would have to be a great shortage of men in the world for Narasimha Pallavar to marry his daughter to a man like him!'

"But had it not been for your grandfather's false predictions, surely he would not cherish this castle in the air?" asked the Shivanadiyar, posing the question slyly.

"And if he did not, the creep would have come after me!" retaliated Valli. "Tell me, is the Pallava princess prettier than our queen?"

"I have given up the world! What do I know about beauty?" said the Shivanadiyar.

"Yes, I can see that you don't know. But if you ever see the Kanchi chakravarti, ask him. When Arulmozhi Devi and King Parthiban were to be married, Narasimha Varman learnt of her loveliness and vowed that he would marry Arulmozhi or become a Buddhist celibate. But Arulmozhi had already agreed to marry Parthiban. And in the end, she did marry Parthiban."

Sly amusement crept across the face of the Shivanadiyar. "And what did Narasimha Varman do after that? Shave his head and convert to Buddhism as a celibate?"

"He married a Pandiyan princess. Do you think a man will keep his word? And a king at that?"

The Shivanadiyar burst into laughter. "You are right! But Narasimha Varman is not such a rogue as you think . . ."

"Let him be a good man then, since you seem to be such a friend of his. Why don't you tell him to marry his daughter to our prince? It would solve all our problems!"

"A good thought, Valli. When you see the Chakravarti next, be sure to tell him."

"Certainly I shall tell him! I am not afraid," said Valli with spirit. At that moment, they heard the splashing of oars dipping into the shallow waters of the dock. "The ferry has arrived," said Valli and went outside.

Counsels and Plots

Arulmozhi Devi and Vikraman entered the hut and prostrated themselves before the Shivanadiyar. The Shivanadiyar affectionately pulled up Vikraman by his shoulders and blessed him. Vikraman had changed. He had been a child when his father died, innocent and naïve. Now, he was a young man, strong and muscular. Character and nobility were written on his face. The keenness of some desire shone in his eyes. He started speaking, the words spilling out one on top of the other. "Swami! Last night, I dreamt my father took me to the temple at Chirapalli and showed me the Pallava flag flying on top. I cannot wait any longer. You must bless me in my effort. I have planned to lower the Pallava flag and hoist the Chola flag."

"You shall always have my blessing. All I have told you is that you must wait until the time is right. I think the time has come. But is the Pallava general Achyuta Varman going to stand hands on hips and let you do whatever you please?"

"My people are ready. Ask Ponnan. He was the organiser. Several warriors will have gathered in Uraiyur on the day of the full moon. When I raise the flag, they will form my army. We will destroy the Pallava regiment and take Achyuta Varman prisoner!"

"Who is assisting you in this dangerous venture? Who is

collecting the troops for you? You are not allowed far from the summer palace . . ."

"My uncle, Marappa Bhupathi, is arranging everything for me–"

The Shivanadiyar cut him off, suspicion lacing his voice. "Marappa Bhupathi knows of this? And he is helping you?"

Vikraman replied enthusiastically, "Uncle Marappa has changed. He regrets the trouble he gave my father and as penance and tribute to him, he is ready to give his life for his country."

The Shivanadiyar glanced at Arulmozhi and said, "Is this true?"

She answered, "Yes, Marappa Bhupathi does seem reformed."

"Well, then, I am pleased with the situation. My blessings. May Kartikeya, leader of the devas, protect you. May Parashakti give your arms strength and your sword speed."

Arulmozhi turned to Ponnan and said, "Ponna! Take the prince to the ferry and wait. I shall come in a moment." Then she turned to the Shivanadiyar and said, "Swami! There are many conjectures as to your identity. But I have never doubted the fact that you have our best interests at heart. Whoever you may be, grant me one boon."

The Shivandiyar's eyes grew soft. "I shall do anything within my power. Ask, my lady!"

"Keep watch over my son. I do not think he will succeed in this venture. He is a boy still. He cannot face the might of the Pallava troops. You have given your blessings. It will be your responsibility to save my son from the danger he shall surely fall into." The queen spoke with great difficulty.

"Only God has the power to save a life, Devi! But I can

promise you this: Vikraman's father's soul shall remain beside his son and keep him safe. Do not worry," the Shivanadiyar replied.

As he spoke, hoofbeats sounded from the west. The Shivanadiyar quickly took his leave and walked away towards the east.

Marappa Bhupathi galloped into the clearing. "Vikrama! Where is the Shivanadiyar? You told me he was coming here today."

"He left just a minute ago," Vikraman replied, indicating the direction in which the Shivanadiyar had gone.

"If he went by this road, I shall catch him soon enough!" said Marappa Bhupathi, jumping on his horse. But though he rode some distance along the bank of the Kaveri, he could not find the Shivanadiyar. He seemed to have vanished into thin air.

Mamallapuram

An air of expectancy pervaded Mamallapuram in anticipation of the Emperor's visit to the city. He was to be accompanied by his daughter Kuntavi. The city was decorated and awaiting their arrival.

The Pallava empire extended from the Kaveri to the Krishna. All the people of this region looked up to Narasimha Pallavar. He was intelligent and valiant, compassionate and just. He was an exponent of music, sculpture and art. Artists flowered and flourished under his patronage. After his victorious campaign to Vatapi his subjects began to feel even greater pride in him. "The land has never seen such a king," the people said. However, he shared a special bond with the citizens of Mamallapuram. After all, he had given the city his name.

The emperor and the princess were seated on the royal elephant. They were surrounded by soldiers. Huge bulls bearing drums led the royal procession. To see the emperor and his daughter at the same time was like seeing the sun and the moon together. There was a light on their faces that came from within.

The emperor of the Pallavas was tall and majestic. Determination, strength and confidence mingled with gentleness on his handsome features. The white, angry scars that ran down his face were testimony to the battles he had fought.

Princess Kuntavi was a distillation of all that was feminine. Artists and sculptors said they forgot their art in the presence of her beauty.

"Father, why was this city given your name?" asked Kuntavi with an air of having asked the question many times before.

"To answer that we'll have to get down from the elephant," replied the Chakravarti.

"Shall I jump?" asked Kuntavi, laughing.

"Were you a common girl, you certainly could," returned her father, joining in the laughter. "You would also be entitled to break your leg doing so. But, as you are my daughter, that privilege is not accorded to you."

Kuntavi pulled a face at him. "Why? Being the Emperor's daughter I am not even allowed to break my leg?"

"Yes. If you were to do so, all the fifty-six princes would refuse to marry you and then I would have to use a trick, like King Janaka did, to get Sita married to Rama."

"What trick? I've not heard of any such story!" exclaimed Kuntavi.

"Don't you know?" asked her father. "When Sita was a little girl, she once lifted a heavy bow not knowing what she was doing. As a result, the kings and princes of fifty-six kingdoms refused to marry her. Finally, you know what Janaka did? He sent Vishwamitra to bring him a silly young prince called Rama. Meanwhile he broke a bow in two and put it together so the joint

was invisible. Rama playfully lifted the bow and it broke into two pieces! Janaka made a big fuss and demanded that Rama either set the bow right or marry his daughter. Rama had no option, he had to marry Sita!"

Kuntavi giggled and said, "But you need have no fear, Father! I hate marriage."

"Why?" enquired her father, laying a long finger thoughtfully upon his nose. "What did it do to you? Such anger for one so young."

"If I marry, I will have to leave you. Since I have no intention of doing that, it is a definite no to marriage. I intend to stick very tightly to you."

"O Lord of the hapless! Merciful protector of the needy! Whichever poor man she is destined to wed, may he avail your protection when she does!" the emperor brought his hands together above his head and gazed prayerfully at the heavens.

"All right. Now, are you going to stop the elephant or not? Or I will try my hand at jumping from elephants, and then nobody will marry me, and I will pester you all my life.'

"That's all I need," said the emperor and motioned to the mahout to stop the elephant.

When it stopped, the two of them got down. The chakravarti turned to the head of the escort and said, "Continue on to Mamallapuram and await us at the gate. We shall meet you there."

Then he mounted his horse, turned away from the highway and cut across the land perpendicular to their destination. His daughter's palanquin followed. No one batted an eyelid. Unpredictability was the rule with the emperor of Kanchi.

The Messenger from Uraiyur

The emperor took Kuntavi to see the rock-cut temples and carved vimanas on top of them. He stopped beside a huge statue of an elephant. "See this? Three years ago, it was a bare, plain rock. Now see how lifelike it is. Thirty years ago when I was like you, my father and I had come here. You know your grandfather was mad about art?"

"And you, of course, are not," his daughter cut in.

"Ah, but he was much worse," returned her father. "He wanted something that would last through the ravages of time. With a piece of chalk I sketched an elephant on a big rock. My father was delighted. He grabbed me and said, "What a wonderful idea, my son! We shall make temples of all these huge rocks. The smaller ones can be made into chariots. We shall make something the world will marvel at, Narasimha, you and I!" He started work almost immediately. For twenty years it went on, nonstop. Then I had to leave for the north, and it just stopped."

The chakravarti stopped and stared into the distance, lost in memory.

Kuntavi waited, then said saucily, "Did the grateful citizens name the city in honour of your having stopped the work?"

The chakravarti laughed. "Since I had the imperial title of

Mahamallan, my father decided to give the city the name Mamallapuram. He loved me so much . . ." And the chakravarti was lost in thought again.

"Yes, but you do not love my brother as much. Else you would not have sent him to Lanka."

"When I was young, I wanted to go on a sea voyage. My father forbade me. As a king, I had no time to indulge myself. So I wanted Mahendran to enjoy what I never did. And that, my dear, is why I sent him off to see the ocean. If I ever loved any other boy like I love him, I would send that one off on a voyage too."

"Had I been born a man," said Kuntavi, "I wouldn't have let you keep the throne so long. No, I would have usurped it in a flash! My brother is a man of peace, poor thing! That's why he obeyed you."

Going from one carving to another, she observed, "Father! These are not finished. Will the work you are coming here to inaugurate include these?"

"No," said her father. "These temples will remain untouched." They began walking to the horses.

Just then, a messenger arrived and, prostrating before the emperor, respectfully handed over a scroll. "Achyuta Varman from Uraiyur sent me with this urgent message," he said.

The chakravarti took the scroll and without even looking at the contents, said, "You may go. I sent instructions about this to Achyuta Varman yesterday." Confused, the man withdrew.

The Festival of Arts

The chakravarti and the princess were in Mamallapuram for three days. On the first day they went about the city so that people could see them. On the next day, which was Saraswati Puja, they set out on a whirlwind tour of all the schools of art. On the third day, which was Vijayadashami, students came to the rocky beach to exhibit their art. Strains of veena, lilting flute and the harmonics of samaveda hymns floated in the air. People wandered from stall to stall, taking in the sights of the tiruvizha, the festival. The chakravarti and Kuntavi also toured the various stalls, stopping briefly everywhere.

The chakravarti gave an attentive ear to each musician — praising some and encouraging newcomers. The sea of humanity that accompanied father and daughter then followed them to the Durga temple and sat under the huge canopy erected in front of it. It was decorated with flowers and mirror-studded drapes. The ministers were ready and as they walked up to their thrones, there were cries of victory and blessings.

The chakravarti tied a silk cloth with his own hands around the head of the chief sthapathi, the chief sculptor. Then he presented him with silk clothing and a hundred gold coins. The ministers did the same for hundreds of other workers.

The Pallava prime minister, Vishnu Sharma, made a short speech celebrating the glory of the Pallava kingdom and Mamalla Chakravarti, whose fame had spread to lands beyond the seas. The assembly burst into spontaneous applause. He announced that the emissaries of the Shenbaga Islands had come to surrender their lands to the Pallava empire.

Vishnu Sharma pointed out that Kanchi and Mamallapuram were the two eyes of the Pallava empire, and elaborated on the importance of Mamallapuram as a seaport and as the economic capital of the empire. He announced that construction work on the beach, which had been halted during Pulikesi's invasion, would resume.

After that, the leader of the deputation from the Shenbaga Islands stepped forward and said, "The inhabitants of the Shenbaga Islands are descendants of the men led by Karikala Cholan on an expedition nearly five hundred years ago. Some years ago, the royal line ended and neighbouring countries began raiding our islands. A council unanimously decided to integrate our land with the Pallava empire as it is the greatest kingdom of our time. We have been sent to ask the emperor to aid us by sending a viceroy to rule us in his name."

The chakravarti did not respond immediately. At length he said that he had not decided his course of action in this matter, and asked for a week's time to reply. After that, he and Kuntavi Devi, with the ministers and artists following close behind, turned their attention towards the temple the chakravarti had come to initiate.

There the emperor began to draw upon the bare outer wall of the temple. Even as the people watched his flying hands, there appeared the lifelike image of Durga, seated upon the lion that was her vehicle, bearing every weapon in her many hands. The emperor turned to the sthapathi and said, "As today is Vijayadashami, what better picture to begin the sculpture with?" The sculptor agreed, took up a chisel and commenced work.

The work they began that day would echo through the ages.

Dilemmas for Kuntavi

Kuntavi was on her way to the temple in Kanchi. She was still thinking of Mamallapuram and the work that would make her father immortal. She knew she was lucky to have such a father. Suddenly, she noticed a young man riding past, surrounded by guards. His face bore the stamp of character and nobility that generally dominated royal bloodlines. Soldiers held thick chains that were bound tight round his body and hands. Though he seemed to be at the end of his strength, the prisoner surveyed the scene calmly, dispassionately, as if to say, "You may bind my body with chains; my mind and spirit are for me alone, that you can never have."

Kuntavi's large eyes widened further at his spirit. At precisely the same moment she spied him, he also saw her. Her beauty stopped him in his tracks for an instant. The next moment, palanquin and horse had passed each other and continued on their separate ways. Kuntavi looked back at the man once or twice. Perhaps she hoped that he, too, would look back at her. But he did not. Whether his chains prevented him from doing so, or his self-discipline, it could not be said.

Kuntavi's concentration was broken. Her thoughts were on the young man she had seen. She finished her prayers quickly.

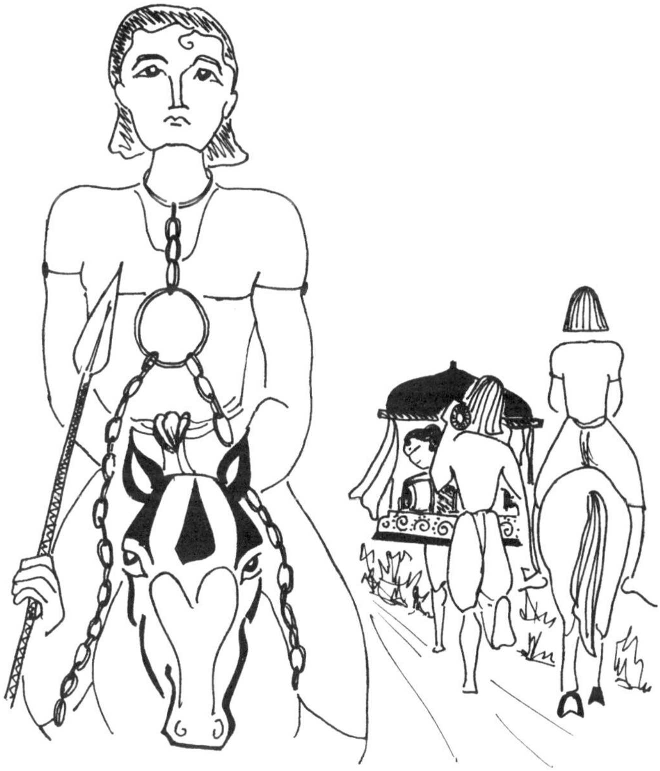

Her father had mentioned something about the Chola prince rebelling against him, and that he had already made arrangements in the matter. Realising that this was the prince, she was angry. "Insolent! That's what he is, insolent and arrogant! To perpetrate such a traitorous deed and pass it off so coolly! To rebel against my father! If he's the one, then I will tell my father to give him a severe punishment. It'll stuff some brains into him!"

Then, remembering the bright face and straight back, she thought, "Poor thing! He didn't look all that bad. He might not have been responsible for what he did. Maybe he was acting under an evil person's influence. He should be warned, counselled and freed. Should I tell father tonight? But there isn't much he doesn't know. He is hailed as the 'Just among kings'. He would not do anything unfair. He will let him go free . . ."

With such thoughts tossing around in her mind, Kuntavi ascended the steps to the palace. Her loyalty see-sawed with her feelings, there was curiosity as well as fear. Sunset and her father's daily visit seemed far away. She sat in her apartments, impatiently counting the seconds to the twilight hour.

A Father and his Daughter

Kuntavi's mother, Vanama Devi, had passed on when Kuntavi was seven. For a while, Sivakami Ammaiyar had looked after her with such love that she barely felt the void created by her mother's death. There was some talk of Sivakami marrying the emperor, but nothing of that sort happened. The chakravarti became both father and mother to Kuntavi. She loved him more than anything else.

As for the chakravarti, his great and joyous heart, which had lain barren for many years, regained its capacity for happiness and love in the person of Kuntavi. Her every word, deed, glance and gesture filled him with delight.

Kuntavi was waiting for her father on the terrace. The moon shone wickedly, beautifully blood-red, between a row of palm trees on the east. But Kuntavi was not interested in such beauty. Her mind was fixed on the young man she had seen on the road. When at last Narasimha Varman joined her, she ran to him.

"You're late," she said accusingly. Her father noticed her unusual eagerness and excitement and was a little surprised.

"I did not take so much time. I came as I always do. Is there something special about today?"

Kuntavi opened her mouth to speak, then shook her head.

"I do have something to say, but that is for later. You tell me. What happened in the court today?"

"Many things! First, there was news from the Lankan islands. The war there was a complete victory. Your brother has asked me what to do about the Lankan king, who has surrendered. He will return soon, but will first go to Madurai to see your uncle. If you wish, you can join him there. Your uncle would love to see you."

"I'm not leaving you. Next?"

"In the Chola kingdom . . ."

"Yes?" Kuntavi asked eagerly, as anticipation coursed through her body. The emperor was surprised, but didn't show it.

"In a place called Kazhi, which is in the Chola kingdom, a boy has been discovered who apparently is enlightened. It is said that he can cure fatal illnesses simply by sprinkling holy ash on the afflicted person. His name is Jnana Sambandar."

"So, a man is emptying the Kingdom of Death? It should be easy — you've not gone on any conquests lately! But wasn't there anything else?"

"Oh, yes, one more thing. When we were in Mamallapuram, a messenger had come, bearing news of a rebellion led by the Chola prince. When I told you about it, you had said that that prince ought to be severely punished. Well, they've brought him here now . . ."

"I saw him on my way to the temple. He passed me by on the road."

Her father blinked. Suddenly, Kuntavi's reactions made sense. He shifted tactics accordingly. "Perhaps it was him," the emperor said carelessly. "Now, dearest daughter, sing one of Appar's songs for me. I love hearing you sing them."

"Where are you keeping him tonight?" persisted Kuntavi.

"In the dungeons, of course!"

"Lord help us!" Kuntavi shrieked.

"What is it? What did you see?" the Emperor asked, pretending to look around for an unseen danger.

"Nothing, Father! I – I was worried he would escape."

Grinning, the emperor said, "Don't worry. If Vikraman tries to escape, he will have twelve Pallava spears through him before he can blink!"

The image this brought before Kuntavi didn't help. "If I tell you something, will you listen to me?"

"Will you let me live in peace if I don't?" her father replied.

"That young man didn't look all that bad. Perhaps someone set him up and egged him on to do what he did."

"True. I was thinking along those lines myself. There is a Shivanadiyar who I suspect was behind this 'uprising'."

"See? I was right! What really happened in Uraiyur? Were many men killed?"

"There wasn't a battle. There wasn't even a skirmish. All that happened was that the idiot was royally fooled and fell happily into our trap," said the chakravarti. "Apparently, he has an uncle called Marappa Bhupathi who led him on with tales of a grand army supporting him. On the day, he wasn't anywhere near Uraiyur. He even informed Achyuta Varman about the attack on the barracks. The soldiers were waiting. The only people who actually were with Vikraman when he was captured were an old man, a boatman, and four or five others. The old man died, the others were captured and Vikraman was brought to Kanchi on my orders."

"Poor thing! He was tricked so basely. But how did you know what was happening?"

"How can you ask such a question, you who know of my psychic powers? And are you going to sing Appar's songs for me or not?" asked the chakravarti, trying mischiveously — and vainly — to change the subject.

"Dear Father, why don't we let him off this time? If I am allowed to speak with that man, I can change his mind. I am sure of it. I can stop him from rebelling against you."

"You can, child, you can." Her father was suddenly serious. "I never said that brainwashing him is not within your capacities. Many women before you have made brilliant men fools and ordinary men geniuses. This is the power of the feminine race.

If you desire, you can make Vikraman forget all about fighting for freedom. But you should have intervened before he committed his crime. Now the culprit must be punished. I can let off Vikraman without penalty today. But can I afford another revolt on the same grounds? Where will this country stand then?"

Kuntavi was helpless before this verbal hurricane. She asked in a small voice, "What will his punishment be?"

"I cannot tell you now, Kuntavi. Tomorrow, when I sit upon the Seat of Justice, what sentence seems fair to me I shall pass upon him. There has never been a Pallava ruler accused of being unjust. It shall not begin with me. It shall never be so, not if I can help it."

At the Docks

That night, Kuntavi had the most terrible nightmares. *Scaffolds have been raised and the prince is going to hang from one of them. She runs towards them, praying to the Goddess for the scaffolds to burn. They flare up in a mighty blaze, and lo, twelve Pallava warriors are going to cut him up with their spears!* Kuntavi woke up and found she had fallen off the bed.

After the third awful nightmare, Kuntavi didn't even attempt to go back to sleep. She kept reminding herself that her father was a merciful man.

When morning came, she tried to speak with her father, but she was just not able to get him alone. As he set out, she felt as if she had to tell him something. "Father!" she called. "Remember what I said!"

Her father turned around and looked at her, puzzled. Then his brows cleared. "What? Oh, the matter about the prince? Of course I remember! You wanted me to punish him well, didn't you?" he said cheerily, and then he was gone.

Fury mingled with sadness in her heart and she collapsed on the bed. When he found out she was the cause of his death, how much he would despise her, she thought and succumbed to a spate of tears. She had to do something. After she had calmed down, she sent for a court official and said to him, "Udaya Varma! When the inquiry of the Chola prince is completed, you shall send someone to tell me what has happened. Immediately!"

"As you command," he replied.

After what seemed an age, a messenger arrived with news of the trial: "Showing the prince great mercy, the emperor granted him a full pardon and the Chola throne if he would swear fealty and pay taxes to the Pallava kingdom. The prince refused to consider the prospect and challenged the emperor to a duel! At that, the emperor delivered a sentence. Taking into his account his youth and courage he was granted his life, and was exiled instead. If he enters the Chola kingdom again, he will be executed forthwith. He was taken to Mamallapuram directly, as the emperor ordered."

Kuntavi was grateful that his life had been spared. But the thought that she would never see him again brought fresh sorrow. She decided to go to Mamallapuram. She was determined that she would see him once more. When she asked for her father, she learned that he had gone off alone on horseback to an unknown location. She summoned Udaya Varman and arranged to leave for Mamallapuram by palanquin.

Even so, the ship was leaving when they reached the docks. Kuntavi felt her heart would break. The prince she had seen on the road the day before was standing on the deck, hands folded together in prayer. He was looking towards the shore. The love, trust and respect that lit up his face made her turn to see whom he was looking at. A Shivanadiyar, with long hair and majestic bearing, stood very straight on the edge of the shore, blessing him.

She looked back at Vikraman. His glance seemed to flicker towards her. Before she could be certain he had seen her, he was looking at the Shivanadiyar again.

Then she remembered that this was probably the man who had prompted the prince to rebel. She went forward to catch him, but the Shivanadiyar dodged behind some workers and disappeared. The ship, when she turned back, had also passed from view.

Ponnan's Doubts

In the chill dawn air, Ponnan was rowing the Shivanadiyar to the summer palace. "So how many of you did reach the barracks with Vikraman?" the Shivanadiyar asked.

"Why speak of that shameful night! If the prince hadn't ordered me to stop . . ."

"What would you have done? Decimated the entire Pallava legion? All by yourself?"

"Yes, tease me, laugh at me. I'm alive, aren't I? I made a promise to the queen, or I would have killed myself for shame long ago. If only I could have died like Virabhadra Achari!"

"What does he have to do with any of this?"

"He was there that night, to see what would happen. He was at a distance from the barracks. He saw the prince deserted and alone, with only five villagers and myself to defend him. He ran to the prince's side, picked up one of the fallen knives, and cried, 'Viravel! Vettrivel! Long live the Chola King Vikraman!' He was nearly eighty, but he killed ten armed soldiers before he died. Achyuta Varman was so awed by the sight that he ordered him cremated with all honours."

"And what happened next?"

"Next? What else? The Pallava warriors surrounded both of

us unawares. I lifted my sword, preparing to swing it — and I heard the prince cry, 'Stop, Ponna!' I looked at him, shocked. He said, calmly, 'There is no use in resisting further. Tell my mother what happened here. Whatever happens, I swear that I shall never act in a manner unworthy of my father. Tell her that.' If anything, I only became angrier. 'I will never leave you in the hands of the enemy,' I cried, and swung my sword wildly without making contact. Someone hit me hard on the head and I woke up in the dungeons. The greatest ignominy was that everyone except the prince was released — and pardoned — by the chakravarti's order!"

"Do you see how good the chakravarti is? Why does your prince rebel against him? Else he wouldn't have been banished."

"Yes, this chakravarti is a great man, and our king is a scoundrel!" Ponnan said, quivering with anger. He paused and then added, "I've never seen the chakravarti. Do you think he might be coming here soon?"

"Yes, I rather think he will. Why, Ponna! What sudden devotion to the emperor has gripped you? You were grieved that you did not die in the war. Now? You have realised the greatness of the chakravarti and worship him!"

"Yes, I am devoted to the chakravarti. You see this spear?" he indicated the weapon lying on the bottom of the ferry. "It, too, is dying to touch him!" And he flourished it.

The Shivanadiyar smiled slyly. "Why point it at me? I'm not the chakravarti, am I?"

Ponnan dropped it. "However good the chakravarti is, he is my mortal enemy. And some day . . . some day . . ." he ground his teeth.

"Where was Marappa Bhupathi that day?"

"Where do you think? Such a traitor would hardly have been anywhere near whatever fighting there was that day. We all fell for his words. Only Valli was stubborn, saying that he was a traitor. And she was right."

"She's a brainy girl. She should have been a general's wife."

Ponnan laughed bitterly. "Marappa Bhupathi said that when he was a general."

"Ah!" the Shivanadiyar said thoughtfully.

"Valli doesn't think you're one of Marappan's men, though."

"I told you, she is one clever woman. She's fit to be a general's wife. When I say that, I also say you're fit to be a general."

"Perhaps I may have been, who knows? But my king has been banished. It was a sentence delivered by a villain. He could have been merciful and killed him . . ."

"Wrong. As long as there is life, one has cause to hope."

The ferry had reached the summer palace. The queen was waiting on the shore.

Ponnan turned towards the Shivanadiyar. "If I have spoken stupidly or rashly, forgive me," he said sincerely as he eased the boat into the shallows.

A Queen's Anguish

When the Shivanadiyar had alighted from the ferry, the queen prostrated before him. She looked up. Tears glistened in her eyes. "Where is my son?" she asked.

"I promised that your son would keep his life. He is alive. I swore he would be as valorous as his father. I have done that too. Had you been in the Kanchi court that day, you would know that what I say is true! The chakravarti tempted your son with sweet words: 'Come within the Pallava Empire, agree to pay a small tax, and you shall have the Chola throne.' Anyone would have fallen under his spell. But your son stood firm as a mountain. He even invited the emperor to a duel! 'If you are the warrior you claim to be,' he said fiercely, 'fight with me, and when I fall dead we shall discuss taxes.' And oh, the light in his eyes as he spoke!"

"And now he is banished to some godforsaken island."

"Besides conquering the land up to the Himalayas, King Parthiban had another dream," the Shivanadiyar continued gently. "Think back on the pictures in the Chitthira Mandapam. He drew the Cholas annexing the lands beyond the sea."

"And is this the fashion in which it is to come true? Vikraman is hardly going on a campaign. He may be in some godforsaken island, at the end of his endurance, just trying to survive! Why are you trying to delude me?" asked Arulmozhi Devi.

"Being exiled to the Shenbaga Islands will give him experience and add to his resourcefulness. When he returns . . ."

"No! He must not return. Execution is the alternative to exile!"

"But he will. Love for his mother and his motherland will draw him back. And another thing. More intense than love for a mother, deeper than the patriotism of a ruler. There is such a force and it has captured him — the eyes of a beautiful woman. I may be one who has no ties in the world, but once long ago, I, too knew the joys and sorrows of love."

"Love? I – I don't understand. What does Vikraman have to do with love or women?" Arulmozhi asked, startled out of her grief.

The Shivanadiyar smiled. "All mothers react like that. My son? And love? What are they to each other? When your son was in Kanchi, he saw a girl on the street. He was bound hand

and foot and was riding a horse when they passed each other. In that instant, the girl fell in love with him. But in Mamallapuram, I saw an astonishing thing. When the ship carrying him away drew out of the harbour, the woman was there. She had come all the way from Kanchi just to see him. Their eyes met, unspoken words passed between them. Her eyes filled with love and compassion. He will never be able to forget them. Day and night, those eyes, that face, shall appear before him. Whatever joy or sorrow comes his way, he will be thinking of that girl, and she will be the one who draws him towards his destiny."

Arulmozhi was stunned. She gathered whatever composure she had and asked, "Who is that woman?" Her voice was soft.

"The Pallava chakravarti's daughter, Kuntavi."

"Oh, Lord! Not my husband's enemy's child! I feel strange. My head! It hurts!" she cried incoherently, and fainted.

The Shivanadiyar asks a Boon

When the queen fainted, the Shivanadiyar sprinkled some water from his kamandalam on her. She opened her eyes and looked up at him.

"You disturbed me by saying that my son loves the daughter of our enemy. O curse me, that I should have such a son!"

"Stop!" the Shivanadiyar said with some bewilderment. He had expected neither the faint nor the outburst. "Consider this: He does not know who she is. He has never spoken to her, never seen her except twice, on the street and at the docks."

"Thank God. I was afraid it was the emperor's plot to make him fall under the witchery of his daughter!"

"Think again, Arulmozhi. Carefully. Did you never wish that the two marry?"

"Perhaps, long ago. But the war changed all that. I can never accept that girl."

"Arulmozhi! You have not seen Kuntavi. I have known her a long time. If you spend a few days with her, you will feel as I do."

"Thank you, no. I have no desire to see or become friends with anyone."

"I have fulfilled my promises to you and your husband. Now, I want you to make me one in return."

"O God!" Arulmozhi got up, bringing her hands together in obeisance. "Why do you step out of custom this far! You need not ask. Command me as to what I should do."

"Some day, Kuntavi could come to Uraiyur. She may visit you. She is a motherless girl. When she comes to you, do not alienate her. Accept her as your own. It will also heal your own wounds." The empathy in his voice thawed the ice in her heart.

"I shall keep my word," she said

"Don't lay the deeds of the father on the shoulders of the daughter. She was my greatest help. She, who never disobeyed her father in word or even thought, fought with him long and hard to free Vikraman. Had it not been for her persistence . . ."

"Perhaps I shall meet her — she has done something for me," said Arulmozhi reluctantly. And the Shivanadiyar smiled enigmatically.

A Sea Journey

The ship that bore Vikraman from his home picked up speed. Soon the land disappeared from sight. The silver froth and brown sand of the seashore vanished and was replaced by dark blue mountains, and valleys. The memory-filled, sorrowful sigh of the sea was loud in his ears.

Vikraman remembered his boyhood dream of sailing into the sunset. He had built in his imagination a huge fleet of ships flying the Tiger flag, bearing warriors waiting to conquer inhospitable lands. It was not a miserable journey as an exile, bound hand and foot, helpless . . . But that was reality.

As he reflected on his plight, a few crew members and the captain removed his chains, apparently on the emperor's orders.

"Where are you taking me?" asked Vikraman.

"To an island twelve days from here. You will remain untied until we reach, but if you attempt to escape, we shall bind you again."

Vikraman remained in the prow and sat watching sea and sky.

He thought of his mother. He wondered how she would bear up under the burden of his exile. The Shivanadiyar would have told her by now. He then thought of the Shivanadiyar.

He reflected on the way he had appeared from nowhere on a horse, leaping down to the docks just as Vikraman was about to leave. What obvious love he had for him! And then, of course, the girl who had appeared mysteriously to bid him farewell. Who was she? And why would a girl he had never seen before come running to meet him? Why did she look at him the way she had?

He sat and thought about her for a long time, long past sunset, in fact. Then he noticed fish darting — it was twilight. Somewhat guiltily, he wrenched his thoughts from her, with an effort, to Ponnan and Valli. They loved him like family.

After a while, the moon rose above the waters. The light that shattered the waves into glittering pearls came from the silver bowl of the three-quarter moon. Vikraman watched it with great interest. Her face had had that same glow. What a contrast it made to the raven locks of her hair! Yes, her beauty was flawless. Neither in picture nor sculpture had he seen that quality, ever. Who was she?

Twelve days passed quickly. On the morning of the thirteenth day, the sun rose, not on the sapphire and gold of the sea, but the emerald and silver of breakers on a lush beach. The captain came up to him. "We have reached our destination. We shall leave you near that island there, with a log to help you float. Do you know to swim?"

"If I refuse to go?"

"Then we will tie you to it and leave you afloat."

A wry smile twisted Vikraman's face. "I'll swim," he said.

The ship drew closer to the beach. Vikraman was put off the side. He could see many people on the beach. Who were they? Were they waiting for him? Why had the chakravarti sent him to this island?

Shenbaga Islands

As Vikraman neared the beach, the sound of the surf was drowned by the music of several instruments. There was also an indistinct shouting that coalesced into a chant: "Viravel! Vettrivel! Viravel! Vettrivel!"

The ancient cry of the Chola empire greatly reassured and vastly surprised him. But his body felt weak and suddenly tired. The log slipped from his grasp. At that very moment, a huge wave hit him at the peak of its crest and flipped him deep into the water. Vikraman felt he had swallowed half the sea and the rest had all fallen on him. Darkness seized him and he knew nothing.

When he returned to life, he was lying on sand. So he was on the beach. He forced his eyes open. Crowds of people bent anxiously over him. There was an eerie silence. "Koo, koo, koo!" The cry of a lone cuckoo broke the silence. More fragments of memory. He had been pulled under the waves as he approached

the seashore. That was probably why the crowd had been so silent. With a mighty effort, Vikraman stood up. The crowd burst out in glad cries. In the midst of all the jubiliation, a big man with a careworn face said stridently, "Make way! Make way for Gajarajan!"

When they heard the voice, people moved aside hastily. A mahout was leading an elephant, all decked to receive royalty. Vikraman stood there, frozen, hands folded, looking at it. When it came to a stop barely inches away from him, he bowed slightly to it. It placed the garland around his neck. The crowd burst into cries. "Viravel! Vettrivel! Viravel! Vettrivel!" "Long live the Chola King Vikraman!" "Long live the lord of the Shenbaga Islands!" and "Long live the king!"

Vikraman had been stunned. What he felt now was too great to be fully felt. By that time, the people had put him on the elephant and it was walking away from the beach. The people made their way behind it, chattering and laughing.

Vikraman felt he was still unconscious. The villages, fields and groves he saw were remarkably like home. When they reached a city, it looked like a smaller Uraiyur, with many palaces and mansions. The people looked like Cholas. Had the Pallava emperor done this to make him see the advantages of his rule?

The elephant stopped outside the largest palace yet. Vikraman was taken down from the elephant. The man who had earlier come to his attention led him towards the interior walls, saying, "My King, this is the ancestral home of the rulers of the Shenbaga Islands. It is our sincere wish that you also take up residence here."

Vikraman felt as if he were in some bizarre dream. "What did you say this place was?" he asked.

"You are on Shenbaga Islands, my king," the man said, a little confused.

"And the name of this city?"

"This is Kumarapuri, the capital."

"And who are you?"

"My name is Siddhartan. I was the minister of the late king."

"Indeed! And how far are we from the mainland?"

"Twelve days' travel at least, my king. With storms or opposing winds, a week more."

"Is that the truth?"

"I speak nothing but truth." Siddhartan looked offended.

"Then how do you, who are surely too far to have regular trade with the Tamil lands, know their language and speak it?"

"Not just on this island, even further south, people speak Tamil. The island was settled by your ancestor, Karikalan. One of his generals ruled for him. That tradition continued until ten years ago, when the last steward died without offspring. Since then, the throne has remained vacant. The neighbouring islands are being pillaged by a strange people. They speak a strange tongue and are very good fighters. They have conquered the nearby areas. You have come to us in our hour of need. It is truly God's grace . . ."

After he mentioned Karikalan's name, Vikraman began paying close attention. Siddhartan's sincerity was obvious. Perhaps it was the weaving of fate that he had come to save what his ancestor had established. "I believe you fully, good sir. I shall hear the rest of the details later. I have only one condition which I must impose if I am to rule here: I shall not pay tax or tribute to any man while I am king. I shall be ruler of a free country, or I shall be a dead man in an enslaved nation. I will hear no talk of submission. Is that clear?"

"My king, the manner of your father's death reached even our distant ears. The people here are fiercely independent — they will sacrifice everything to remain free. All we need is a leader who can take us to victory." He smiled. "And we have one. What else do we want?" A bell tolled in the distance, calling Vikraman to his coronation.

Kuntavi's Oath

The chakravarti and his daughter Kuntavi Devi were seated on the flower-filled terrace of their palace in Kanchi. It was a star-studded night. Far, far south, just at the edge of their vision, the light of the lighthouse at Mamallapuram also shone, a brighter light in the horizon. "Are you well, my child?" the emperor asked. "You certainly don't look it."

"Nothing wrong with my body. It is the heart that troubles."

"This heart of ours!" the emperor said cheerfully. "It is a very deceitful thing. It's like a mad elephant, say the elders. They say it must be tamed by the angusha, the controlling stick, of the mind."

"How did you know I went to meet the leader of the Shamana sect?"

"If I do not know what my one and only darling daughter is doing, how am I supposed to rule a vast nation where I have to know what everyone's doing?"

"Father, I am going to join the Shamanas or the Buddhists. I have lost interest in life."

"That bad? What have the Shaiva and Vaishnava sects done to you — or to themselves?"

"There is no joy in life for me any more. I wonder why I was ever born into this miserable world."

The chakravarti burst out laughing. Oh, he laughed very richly! Kuntavi turned away from him, exasperated and annoyed.

"A long time ago, I was just like you. I, too, was tired of life. Do you know why?"

"Because I was born?"

"No, not at all. In fact, your birth was what brought some light into my existence. Before that I had hated life. Why? Because I was angry with my father!" he said with mock solemnity. Seeing a smile push itself unwillingly onto Kuntavi's face, he continued. "Isn't that why you are out of sorts with life?"

Tears glimmered in Kuntavi's eyes. She wiped them. Head bent, she said, "I think that your action in exiling the prince was a little hasty, Father. If it were proved that the Chola prince's actions were not his own, would you change the sentence?"

"Undoubtedly! If I have adequate proof, I would rectify the error immediately."

"I will find that pretender Shivanadiyar and turn him over to my father, I swear!" Kuntavi thought to herself.

"What deep thoughts are you submerged in, Kuntavi? I said I am going to Uraiyur in two days. Are you coming?"

"Of course! I want to see Arulmozhi Devi."

"Will she want to see you? I was the one who exiled her son, you know."

"What does that have to do with my wanting to visit her? Was I the one who exiled him? Did I urge him to betray his rightful ruler? What's the use of being angry with me!"

"There's no telling with women!" the chakravarti thought to himself. "Blood ties evidently has no meaning for them! They're unfathomable!"

Ponnan's Humiliation

Thunder, lightning, earthquake and fire had wracked the little house for three days. "I told you once, I've told you a thousand times, I made a mistake, I'm sorry! Why can't I be given some peace and allowed to live in honour? What's your problem with a quiet existence!" Ponnan protested hotly.

"What's the use of saying sorry, sorry, sorry, now? What happened to your brains then?" said Valli, even more hotly.

"So what has happened now that you are shouting at me like this, Valli? Where is that emperor? Where can he go? Where is my spear!" Ponnan's face was red.

"A spear? A spear!" Valli looked to the heavens. "You want a spear? You might stab yourself with it by mistake! Your hands, dear husband, were made to clutch an oar and beg favours from enemies. How can a hand which lies folded in obeisance hold a spear?"

What had happened was this: Two days earlier, the emperor and his daughter Kuntavi had come to the docks on their way to Uraiyur. The chakravarti was pointing to the roof of the palace that was just visible in the distance and saying something to Kuntavi. His gaze fell on Ponnan and Valli, who were standing at the door of their cottage. He beckoned Ponnan with a gesture.

Ponnan ran to him, prostrated, and then stood with his hands tucked respectfully. He completely forgot that he was supposed to have taken revenge when he saw the emperor next, he did not remember that his spear was to have made a home in the emperor's chest. When he saw the chakravarti, that knowing smile and the aura of power that he radiated, Ponnan was speechless.

"Are you the boatman of this dock?" asked the Chakravarti. Ponnan lost what wits he had left.

"Yes, my kin – chakra – lord!" he managed to get out.

"Look here. My child Kuntavi will want to come later to visit Arulmozhi Devi. When she does, you will personally ferry her to the island, do you understand?"

"I understand, my lord!" replied Ponnan. And then the chakravarti had gone away towards Uraiyur.

Valli had been listening to some of the conversation, and that was enough. When Ponnan returned to the hut shamefacedly, she was seething with fury. She began yelling at him. She accused him of being a traitor. Ponnan was hapless under this whirlwind of allegations, but insisted that he had not meant it. Valli continued to yell. It was three whole days now and she was still yelling.

Ponnan couldn't take any more. He retreated to the riverbank and sat thinking vengeful thoughts. The fresh, rain-washed leaves only served to heighten his anger. The dock had been a busy place ten years ago. The king and his family had always been coming and going. Now? Parthiban was dead on a battlefield. Arulmozhi was breaking her heart in the summer palace. Vikraman was languishing on some godforsaken island. Not a soul came from or went to the palace. He was sitting here taking insults from Valli, and life was not worth living. None of this would have happened had it not been for that – that cretin, Marappa Bhupathi. If that traitor hadn't told Achyuta Varman, Vikraman would have driven out the invader and ascended the throne by now. The chakravarti would not have come to Uraiyur. And he would have had some peace of mind instead of having to face a storm every time he stepped over his threshold.

While he was thinking all this and wondering what would happen when he eventually had to go back to Valli, he heard the sound of hoofbeats. He turned around in time to see Marappa Bhupathi alight from his horse and go into the hut.

Marappan's Desires

Ponnan followed Marappan into his house. When Marappan saw Ponnan, he said, "Ah, Ponna! I wanted to talk to you." So they went out again and sat under a tree on the river-bank.

"Ponna," said Marappan, "you have done me a great favour. I must pay off that debt someday."

"Oh God! Don't tell Valli this, she'll make life hell for me."

Marappan laughed, and said, "You did me a great favour by marrying Valli! I wanted to, once, you know. I shudder to think what I would have had to bear as her husband!"

"Of course. Your pacifist nature and her boldness would have been quite incompatible. Everyone knows you get a fever at the mere mention of war."

"What did you say?" hissed Marapppan. His knife came out from its sheath in a flash of steel.

"So! Your knife is real! I must tell Valli. She wagered quite a bit that your knife is made of wood. I shall fetch her." And Ponnan got up.

Marappan placed the knife on the ground beside him. "Don't drag a woman into this. This is men's work, Ponna. Remember how all our efforts to reinstate Vikraman went for naught because Arulmozhi Devi was with us? She insisted on telling the Shivanadiyar, who told Achyuta Varman."

When Ponnan heard about the Shivanadiyar, his doubts resurfaced. Had he suspected Marappan wrongly? He felt a little guilty.

"Whoever it is," he growled, "when the truth comes out, I will . . ." He ground his teeth. Seeing Marappan's knife lying near him, he picked it up and hurled it into a tree next to Marappan's head. It went in very deep. Marappan shivered involuntarily.

"We've not lost anything, Ponna. The past is over but the nation remains. As long as you and I are still there, nothing need be abandoned. What we cannot do by war we can accomplish by peace. You are a smart one, Ponna! When the chakravarti came here, you behaved with proper respect. Let foolish women like Valli babble on. If you help me, we can salvage the kingdom and keep it for Vikraman."

Though the words were persuasive, Ponnan found it difficult to believe him.

"How am I supposed to help?" he asked cautiously.

"When Princess Kuntavi comes, row her across and tell her all about me. You remember the future foretold to me by Valli's grandfather? Well, it's coming true. Why else would Kuntavi come here now?"

Ponnan thought briefly about Arulmozhi Devi's wish that Kuntavi and Vikraman marry. It refuelled all his anger towards Marappa Bhupathi. Without showing a trace of it, however, he replied, "Is that all? When the time comes, you can be sure I will tell her all about you."

"I will not easily forget your help. I am going to Uraiyur to meet the emperor. He will give me the post of general. And I will take good care of you." He got onto his horse and trotted away.

In the Emperor's Sanctum

When Ponnan told her about his conversation, all of Valli's anger turned towards Marappan. "So the fool wants you to be his ambassador for the Kanchi princess, does he? If he had asked me to do the same, I would have upturned a pot of live coals on his head!"

Ponnan protested, saying, "I threw his own knife at him, only there was a tree between us." But Valli took some convincing.

They discussed what they would do next. They had decided that they had to tell the emperor about Marappa Bhupathi. But how were they going to get to him?

"You spoke to him the other day, didn't you? Well, just walk up there and do it again," was Valli's contribution.

"Everyone in Uraiyur knows I was associated with the revolt. If I said I was going to see the emperor, I'd be in the dungeons before I could say 'Marappa Bhupathi'," said Ponnan. And so on and so forth.

Then they heard horses slowing to a stop at their doorstep. "Now who is it?" they wondered as they went outside — and stopped short as they saw six fully armed Pallava warriors on horseback.

"Boatman, we are ordered to bring you to the august presence of the Pallava chakravarti," said their leader. "Will you come with us civilly, or must we be crude and tie you across the saddle?"

Ponnan looked at Valli, confused by the sudden command. She said boldly, "Respect is given in the Chola kingdom to all, no matter how lowly. Perhaps respect goes around in quarter rations in your kingdom. Who knows?"

"I judge by your sweet words that you are Valli, the insolent woman. You are also to be brought to the emperor."

And so they were on the way to meet the emperor. They had surmised that he wanted them to testify on Marappan's role in the revolt. When they heard Marappan's whining voice in the emperor's chamber, they knew they had inferred correctly. A rich, deep voice commanded, "Bring the boatman in!"

Ponnan and Valli were taken into the room.

The emperor was seated upon a bejewelled throne. Kuntavi Devi was leaning casually against the wall. Marappan was cowering in front of the throne. They took all this in at a single glance. Then their heads bowed instinctively before the emperor's face. He looked close to erupting in fury.

The chakravarti spoke in a tone of quiet anger, like a thundercloud in the distance. "So! This is the boatman? We saw him at the docks. He made a convincing performance of being a meek person! If even he rebels against his ruler, well, what can I say about the state of the empire?"

Whatever bravado Ponnan and Valli had accumulated on the way vanished entirely.

The chakravarti continued, scowling. "Let that rest, I shall deal with that later. Now, boatman! I shall ask you a few questions.

Raise your head and answer. Raise your head! Now, tell me, who was responsible for the attack on the barracks?"

Ponnan raised his head and said brightly, "Why, this man, here. The one in front of you. Marappa Bhupathi!"

Valli's Curses

When he heard Ponnan's words, Marappan jumped as if he'd been stung by a few hundred scorpions. Then his eyes returned to inspecting the carpets and studiously avoiding the emperor.

"And what have you to say, Bhupathi?" The thunder was closer now. Marappan jumped again.

"My Emperor, Lord! What this man says is utter falsehood. I pretended to go along with their plan for a while so I could learn the details before I reported to Achyuta Varman. I have served you long and faithfully . . ."

"*Traitor! Oh, you miserable creep!*" said a mysterious voice.

"Who said that?" demanded the emperor sharply. The voice seemed to have come from somewhere near Valli. But she stood demurely, head bowed.

Marappan screwed up his courage and said, "My Lord! This fool was not the reason behind Vikraman's actions. I know there is someone else. I can tell you! If I may," he added belatedly.

"Do!" said the emperor icily.

"It is a Shivanadiyar. He has long hair and a beard. He occasionally visited Arulmozhi Devi and Vikraman. He was the one who spurred Vikraman on to such heinous deeds."

"And how do you know this?" asked a new voice. It was

Kuntavi, who had snapped upright from her casual pose against the wall.

"I have seen him. He often met with the queen and the prince at that man's house." He indicated Ponnan. "I have tried several times to expose him for what he is, but these people here, this Ponnan and Valli, prevented me."

"*If you speak of me, I shall slice your tongue out*," the earlier voice said, softly and dangerously.

The chakravarti turned to Valli. "I have observed your lips moving several times, girl. Speak freely."

She bowed and said, "This man has been spouting lies all this time, my lord. The Shivanadiyar did not egg Vikraman on. The Shivanadiyar is a good man. He came often to console the queen and her son. He told the prince several times that it was a

foolish venture. He could not change Vikraman's mind. Anyone who accuses the Shivanadiyar is a rogue and will surely go to hell!"

"Stop! Enough cursing, girl, calm down!" said the emperor, amused. He turned to face Kuntavi, grinned roguishly and said, "See, my lady?"

"I saw. I heard, too. I use my wits sometimes," said Kuntavi, singularly unimpressed. "None of them has told the whole truth."

The chakravarti turned around again to face Marappa Bhupathi, his temper performing one of its infamous switches. Marappan cowered under his fury. "Bhupathi! The charges against you have not been cleared. I shall give you the benefit of doubt — this time. You have clearly proved that the post of general is beyond your capacities. Until you convince me that you are even a little fit to hold any post of responsibility, you will see to it that no other accusations are levelled against you." The emperor leaned towards him. "Is – that – clear?"

Marappan gulped and left the room.

A man entered quietly and handed the emperor a message. The emperor read it and said, "Ferryman! You and your wife can go now. I shall see to you later. Oh, and tell your wife to be a little careful where that Shivanadiyar is concerned. She seems quite enchanted by him."

Valli blushed, embarrassed. Then suddenly she smiled. There was a look of amazement on her face. She gazed intently at the emperor. She left the room still looking back at him, knowingly, respectfully.

The emperor said to Kuntavi, "We were discussing a false Shivanadiyar. Now we have a real one coming to visit us. It's Paranjyoti Adigal."

"Your old general? The one who went with you to Vatapi to conquer Pulikesi?" asked Kuntavi.

"He didn't just come with me — he was the one who fought with Pulikesi when the northerners were pouring out of the city like ants from a hill. He calls himself a siruthondar now, and has taken sanyasa. Do you want to come with me to meet him?"

"Certainly!" said Kuntavi.

The Siruthondar

They waited for the siruthondar in a mandapam by a lovely lotus pond on the west side of the Kaveri. The chakravarti and Kuntavi were seated on its edge, their guards standing discreetly behind them. The chakravarti was watching the east road intently.

"Kuntavi! I see them!" her father's voice rang with joy. "They're on their way! Can you see the procession? My friend, the Pallava general, the warrior who killed Pulikesi at Vatapi, he comes! You see how fortuitous our arrival at Uraiyur was?"

The chakravarti was grinning from ear to ear. Kuntavi was astounded. She had never seen her father as delighted as he was now.

A short while later, the palanquin crossed the pond. When the bearers saw the emperor standing there, they hastily set it down. A man who looked to be middle-aged got out. His head and face were completely shaven and his forehead was smeared with ash. He wore a string of rudraksha beads round his neck. An old woman was with him.

He came towards the mandapam, saying, "Sire!" and at precisely the same moment the chakravarti ran down the steps saying, "Senatipati!" The two met near the bottom of the steps and appraised each other for a while. Then, as of one accord, they fell into an embrace. Both were crying openly. When the emperor and his friend separated from their embrace, they stood close, looking at each other.

"See? I was truly fortunate in coming to Uraiyur at this time. If I hadn't, I might have missed you. You're the one who's forgotten me. When was the last time you came to Kanchi?" the chakravarti said.

"As if anyone could forget you! I remembered you at every single shrine that I visited in the south. I always wished you were beside me, and I always regretted that you were not. Wherever I went, you were the only thing I ever desired. And now, I've met you," replied the siruthondar.

"Senatipati –"

"Do not address me as that, sire! I put that behind me a long time ago."

"Paranjyoti –"

"That, too, I left when I came on this voyage. I am but a siruthondar, servant of the enlightened."

"All right, Siruthondar, now listen. I have only two things to do, two promises to fulfil. After that, I'm free as a bird. But don't even think I'm going to shave myself bald. I, in the tradition of Vasishta, shall have long hair, a moustache and a beard!"

The birds were returning to their nests in the darkening evening. The emperor began laughing, and his old friend laughed with him. One rich, and the other lilting, the two tones rose delightedly into the dusk.

At Midnight

Uraiyur was eerily silent and deserted, and long shadows fell across the streets. The lamps which lit up the street corners dimmed and sizzled in the light rain, the oil running out. Ponnan was dragging a boat along the banks. Valli sat in the boat.

At a distance of about a hundred feet behind them was a dark figure cautiously trailing the boat. When the boat stopped, the figure stopped, and when it moved on, the figure moved forward as well. The figure was none other than Marappa Bhupathi.

Roughly at the same distance behind the shadowy form of Marappan followed yet another, silent form. This was the Shivanadiyar.

It was around midnight when Ponnan called out to Valli in a whisper that they had arrived. The door to the royal garden was heavily padlocked. Ponnan took a ring of keys from his belt and opened the lock with a key. The door creaked open ominously and they went inside.

"Valli! Isn't the smell of the shenbaga flowers lovely? This is your first time in the royal garden, is it not?" Ponnan asked loudly.

"Be quiet!" hissed Valli.

Ponnan shut the door and locked it from the inside. "Don't be afraid. I'm with you," he said encouragingly.

"The only thing I am afraid of is that you will get us caught by yelling!" replied Valli. Suitably subdued, Ponnan led Valli on through the garden.

A little while later, Marappan walked out of his hiding place. He climbed the steps to the building and locked the door from the outside. He came back down and untied the boat, letting it float away. Then he climbed the steps again and vanished round the corner.

A little while later, the Shivanadiyar walked out of his hiding place. He climbed the steps to the building and unlocked the door. He came back down and tied the boat up where he caught it. Then he sat down near the boat. Even in the darkness, his eyes pierced the wall keenly and his ears listened for any sound.

Marappan is Confused

Marappan had left the emperor's chamber angry and bitter. All the service he had rendered the Pallava Empire for seven years had gone waste! He had been patient. He had served. All he wanted was to rule his country under the Chakravarti. Even the post of general would have sufficed. And what had happened? The chakravarti had doubted him. Doubted him! Besides, he had been humiliated in front of a mere boatman and that wife of his!

He rode around aimlessly. His horse, taking advantage of the loose reins, meandered where it wished, and soon was trotting along on the road between Uraiyur and Srirangam. Marappan was busy thinking.

They had travelled a fair distance before he realised where he was. Cursing, he turned the horse back towards Uraiyur. When he had entered the fortress of Uraiyur, he heard a great blowing of horns and conches and drums heralding a procession. He saw the Lion flag flying, but when they came closer, he saw with some relief that the emperor was not with them. Achyuta Varman was at the head of the procession accompanied by a clean-faced, shaven-headed sanyasi.

As they went past, Marappan noticed a palanquin surrounded

by women coming straight at him. It stopped and a sweet voice from within summoned him: "Bhupathi!"

When he realised that it was Kuntavi who had called out to him, his heart bounded with delight and surprise.

"Bhupathi! My father treated you harshly today. Do not worry. I believe what you said. Just find that false Shivanadiyar. Hand him over to my father. And then I will be on your side in this matter."

Hearing her address him so affectionately, Marappan was overjoyed. He looked up at the bottom of the palanquin and replied, "Devi, I shall not rest or sleep until that Shivanadiyar is brought to justice!"

The palanquin moved on at a soft word from Kuntavi.

Even after the procession had moved on, Marappan stood rooted to the spot. He thought about the bald sanyasi who had been with Achyuta Varman. He knew that Paranjyoti had been a good friend of Parthiban. Was this the fugitive Marappan was looking for? He would need Ponnan and Valli's help in this matter. And so Marappan took the straightest path to the street of blacksmiths.

As he turned the corner, he saw a sight in the light of the dying lamp which stopped him dead and petrified him — it was a man about to turn the corner. Not just any man, though. Just as he recovered his wits and sprang forward, the light went out and the street was plunged in darkness. He gave chase in the direction the man had taken. When he reached the place where he had spotted him, the Shivanadiyar had disappeared! There were, as if everything else were not enough, four streets he could have gone down.

Then he thought that the fugitive had probably come to talk

to Ponnan and Valli. If so, he could catch them red-handed and take them in to the emperor. Just then, he saw the door of Virabhadra Achari's house open. Ponnan and Valli came out. She held a hooded lamp. Filled with glee at the thought that he would catch them and that infernal Shivanadiyar red-handed at something, he slunk behind them. They went into the royal gardens. Marappan was convinced that they had gone in to perpetrate another crime, and that the Shivanadiyar was in there with them.

Anyway, all the mysteries would be solved tonight. It was with this thought that he locked the door of the garden and went off to get his men.

The Saviour

Blissfully unaware that two different men were shadowing them, Ponnan and Valli walked through the royal garden. Now and then, Ponnan stopped to tell Valli something in a loud voice, each time to be admonished by her. The strange voices in the middle of the night woke a few birds and they fluttered and squawked irritatedly. Ponnan patted his wife's hand comfortingly. "Sshhh!" he said loudly to the birds.

"All your bravery seems restricted to birds sleeping in the night. If you see a knife in an enemy's hands, you will probably fall over fainting and come home to lick your wounds!" said Valli, annoyed. That, she noticed with some satisfaction, shut him up.

Ponnan took her to the east side of the palace. They entered the Shiva temple. Ponnan went over to the shrine of Vishnu and picked up a long, plain box that lay at its feet.

"This, Valli, is the heritage of the Chola kingdom. Luckily, that Narasimha Varman didn't see it, or it would be in Kanchi before we could blink!" Ponnan said as he came out of the temple. Valli followed him. Then he heard her gasp in dismay, "Oh! the light's gone out!"

"Well, at least it waited until we finished our work! All right.

Now how do you want to go out? The garden path is difficult to go by in the dark. We can go through the entrance gate of the palace. Let me check whether it's open."

As they were going to rattle the lock to see if it was bolted, they heard voices from the other side of the fence and froze.

"Why are we sitting here sharpening knives?" they heard someone say.

"Because Marappa Bhupathi is the greatest fool in the world, and we have to agree when he says that there are thieves in the palace, because he is our commander! Why would a thief come here?"

"What's that there? Looks like a lot of torches," came another voice.

"Must be Marappa Bhupathi with the rest of the troops," was the reply.

Ponnan paled. His knees nearly buckled when he heard what was being said. His mind darted in a thousand different directions. He saw Marappan catching him red-handed, the box in his hands. He saw himself taken before the emperor. He grabbed Valli's hand and the two of them raced towards the north gate, the Kaveri, and escape.

They tripped over creepers and bumped into trees and fell over roots. They ran until they reached the outer gates. There they stood still, listening. When they heard no noises, they cautiously opened the gate and went outside. And received their next shock. The boat was gone!

For one awful second they couldn't even breathe. The torches were so close now that they could be seen even through the thick growth. Then Ponnan said quickly, "It's probably gone downstream. Come on!"

A crowd of men was coming through from the east side of the palace. "There they go!" someone shouted.

Ponnan and Valli ran even faster. Then they saw, stunned, that their boat was tied to another tree. But this was not the time to be astonished. The men were coming closer. Ponnan was in agony, thinking they were going to be captured with the incriminating box in their hands. Just then, a dark form emerged from the shadows. Valli cried out in startled joy when she saw that it was the Shivanadiyar.

"Quiet," he said, authoritatively. "Ponna! This is not the time to be exchanging polite words. Give me that box. I'll return it to you later. If you do not give it to me, you will get caught. I, on the other hand, can escape these men easily. Give it to me."

"He's right, let him have it," whispered Valli with conviction.

Ponnan hesitated. Then he reached out to the Shivanadiyar and gave him the box.

"I repay my debts," said the Shivanadiyar. "Farewell!" He took two decided steps backward into the forest and simply — vanished. Ponnan dragged the boat into the water and he and Valli got into it.

It was at that moment that Marappan's men reached the bank of the Kaveri, and Marappan's confusion began again.

Celebrations

Poor Marappan had arrived too late as usual. He saw Ponnan's boat streaking out and started to shout: "Stop that boat! Catch those two and tie them up! Don't let them past! Search the boat!"

His men darted this way and that. Ponnan and Valli came back obediently and let Marappan's men search them and the boat. Marappan even made his men search the river. There was nothing.

"Where is it? Where is it? Where is it?" he asked, turning viciously on Ponnan.

"Where is what?" asked Ponnan innocently.

For the next few, definitely unprofitable, minutes, Marappan cajoled and babbled and blurted. Finally he threatened. "You entered the palace, and you came out with something, and you have hidden it here somewhere. Tell the truth! You have stolen something. Confess to it right now, or I shall throw you in the dungeons!"

"Which you have the authority to do? And where would you do it?" Ponnan asked mockingly.

Valli chimed in, "Why talk to him? Let him put us in prison. We shall see about these things when we go on trial before the emperor tomorrow."

That deflated Marappan. He said in a conciliatory tone, "Ponna, let us be friends as we have always been. All I ask of you is one little thing. About that false sanyasi. Tell me where he lives and when I catch him I shall find favour for you at the court. I have sworn to do so in front of the emperor's daughter. If I catch him, I shall soothe the princess's anger against you, which is considerable."

"I couldn't reveal the Shivanadiyar's location even if I wanted to."

"Did you know that he was in Uraiyur this very evening? Can you deny that?"

"How can I say that? The swami is possessed of great powers — he can be here one minute and there the next," said Valli cheekily.

"So you do not know the Shivanadiyar's hiding place?"

"No," replied Ponnan and Valli, in unison and with perfect truth.

"Forget what I said earlier. I swear I will track that man down and I will yank off his wig and find out who he is. And I won't let you off then either." Glowering, Marappan stalked off.

"You know," said Valli the next day, "If he actually pulls the Shivanadiyar's beard off and sees his face, he'll faint!"

"I don't know who he is either!"

"Tell me what's in the box and I'll tell you who he is."

"The box is a box of wonders. It holds the manuscript of the Tirukkural and the sword of Karikal Valavan and Nedumudikkilli. The queen wanted it to be safe from the Pallavas and she asked me to bring it to her. That's why I didn't want to give it to the Shivanadiyar. What if I never see it again? How can I tell the queen? You were the one who forced me into it," said Ponnan.

"What did I do? In that moment, there was nothing else we could do, and well you know it. But somehow, I am certain it will come back unharmed," said Valli.

"Well, it's good if it does. Otherwise, we can't show our faces to the queen. But you haven't told me yet. Who is the Shivanadiyar?"

Valli whispered something in her husband's ear. His eyes widened in surprise. He was about to reply, then broke off. There was a sound of horses galloping towards them. They went to the door.

A Flood of Tears

When Valli and Ponnan came out of their home, they beheld an astonishing sight. A royal procession was coming down the road from Uraiyur. At the same time, several boats were coming down the Kaveri, also from Uraiyur. The Lion fluttered proudly at their helms. When he saw the flag, Ponnan realised that it was the emperor himself coming with his attendants.

As he waited for the boats to turn towards the docks, another surprising thing happened. The boats turned towards the summer palace.

Ponnan walked over casually to the soldiers and enquired why the emperor was visiting the island. The soldier said that the emperor, his daughter, and the siruthondar and his wife were visiting the queen.

Ponnan wished he could go to the queen. When he told Valli this, she said sharply, "Really! Do you really think they'd let you go there? Events will reveal themselves. Be patient."

So he remained fretting and fuming for half an hour. Finally there was some sign of activity on the island. People assembled at the dock on the other side and began climbing into the boats and coming over the river. The lead ship held the proud form of the chakravarti and with him, a bald sanyasi.

Then their eyes fell to the next boat, which held three women. The first was Kuntavi, the next a saintly lady, a Shivabhakta. At the third, their breath caught. It could not be — but it was — the regal form of Arulmozhi Devi.

Yes. It was truly she. The boats docked. Transfixed, they stood, gazing at the queen. Simply looking, looking at her face.

She came to them, compassion in her eyes. "Ponna! Valli! I cannot stay here any longer. I am going on a pilgrimage with the siruthondar and his wife. Don't worry about me. Just stay here, at this peaceful dock by the Kaveri. Who knows, I might even return some day . . ."

She stopped. Ponnan's eyes and Valli's too were brimming with tears. Her own filled as well. She held the elderly lady's hand, seeking sustenance, and they walked off down the road together.

The group travelling east left first. The siruthondar got into a palanquin alone. His wife and Arulmozhi Devi climbed into another. They had gone some distance when Ponnan was struck by a sudden thought. He darted down to the ladies' palanquin. When Arulmozhi saw him, she asked the bearers to stop and enquired, "Ponna! What is it? You look flustered."

"Devi! We were discussing a certain box the other day," he said.

"Have you found it?" the queen leaned out and asked eagerly.

"Yes – no, we will soon." Ponnan hit a blank again.

The queen was silent for a while. Then she said, "Ponna! If you find it, keep it safe. If I do not return, and he comes home . . ." Arulmozhi's eyes flooded, and she began weeping softly. The carriage passed on.

As Ponnan was heading for his home, he saw that the chakravarti's horse and his daughter's palanquin were still there.

Kuntavi was crying, he saw, and the emperor was comforting her. Across the distance that separated them, he heard her say, brokenly, “I thought I had found a mother, Father. I was so happy. And even she has left me now.”

She got into her palanquin and her father sprang onto his horse. They set off towards Uraiyur.

Ponnan walked into his house and found his wife sobbing. “If only I’d known,” Valli wept. “What do I have here? I would have gone with her, if only I’d known!”

Steeling himself, Ponnan said, “See? Now you speak like a woman.”

Then they heard the clip-clop of horses again and they went outside. The emperor was on his stallion in front of their hut. He was alone. “Ponna! Will you be staying here?”

“Yes, my Lord!”

“Good. I have ordered my men to leave the royal boat on this side of the river. If my daughter desires to stay in the summer palace, you will ferry her both ways. Understood?”

“Yes, my lord. I shall await her.”

“Another thing. I have a friend — a Shivanadiyar — who gave me a box to give you. I think you will find it in the bottom of your boat.” He said the last sentence looking straight at Valli. She ducked her head bashfully, but Ponnan caught a sly grin on her face.

The next moment, the emperor had wheeled his horse around, and the stallion he rode was streaking down the road back to Uraiyur in a cloud of dust.

BOOK THREE

The Jewel Merchant

Vikraman was coming home. After three years of exile and three years as the king of Shenbaga Islands, he could no longer bear to be away from his own country. The land and his mother beckoned.

He had acquitted himself as an able ruler and general. He had dealt successfully with attempts to invade the Islands, and his people were secure. There was prosperity, and small neighbouring kingdoms sought his protection and patronage.

Two months ago, Vikraman had had a dream in which his mother had come dressed in the white robes of a Shivabhakta and told him that she had promised the Shivanadiyar that Vikraman would marry Kuntavi, the Pallava princess! Vikraman had woken up with a feeling of disbelief, but the dream had made him extremely homesick and he found himself finding all kinds of reasons to go back to Uraiyur. He was a free king now and had the right to retrieve the box with the Tirukkural and the sword of the Cholas. He wanted to see his mother and bring her back to live with him.

There was something else as well. Unbidden, Vikraman's thoughts wandered to the lady at Kanchi and the expression on her face when his ship had set sail. He decided he could wait no more. After cajoling his ministers into letting him go by promising to return with a queen, he set sail for the mainland posing as a jewel merchant.

He set sail for Mamallapuram. He had always wanted to see the temples and sculptures there. He also thought that perhaps he would be able to lure some artisans and masons to Shenbaga Islands. Then again, maybe, deep down, there was a desire to see the mysterious woman again.

Many Meetings

It was three years almost to the date of Vikraman's exile, and the festival of arts and music was in full swing at Mamallapuram. The emperor of Kanchi had not come to attend the festival. It was being said that he had relinquished his duties to his son, Mahendra Varman, who had now returned from Lanka, while the emperor was roaming the country in disguise. However, since Mahendra Varman and Kuntavi Devi were now in Mamallapuram, the citizens continued their merrymaking.

Vikraman wandered the streets, soaking in the atmosphere, eagerly taking in the music, the dances, the sculptures, the carvings and drawings. There was a glow on his face, boundless happiness in his eyes. Nothing had prepared him for *this*! His craving for beauty satiated itself and grew at the same time. Music was doing for his ears what art was doing for his eyes.

A gnarled old man, not fully grown — his name was Chitragupta — shuffled along behind the jewel merchant, carrying his bags. He could neither speak nor hear and it was for that reason precisely that Vikraman had picked him when he landed at Mamallapuram. He did not want anyone to hear what he said. Ever so often, after having scrutinised an artist's work, Vikraman would take him aside and talk to him about the

Shenbaga Islands and the opportunities available there. He presented a gem as token payment if they agreed to accompany him back. As it was a major offence to suborn artists or lure them to other countries, Vikraman exercised great discretion.

On the third day of the festival, which was Vijayadashami, he heard a commotion. He turned around to see what it was about and beheld a palanquin heading down the street with her in it. She had changed. She seemed more beautiful than ever but there seemed to be some unspoken sorrow reflected in her eyes. His heart pounded against his chest. He had rehearsed this scene thousands of times in his mind, but every possible thought flew out of it at that moment. He simply moved to the side of the

street like everyone else and turned away from the palanquin that was approaching him.

As the palanquin went by, he felt, unmistakably, a large dark pair of eyes focusing in his direction. He had a strong impulse to turn back and meet those eyes but he resisted, and the palanquin went past. He heaved a sigh and looked up and back at the retreating palanquin . . . only to find that the eyes had not, after all, left him and that the woman was still gazing right at him. Their eyes met for a second and then he quickly turned away his gaze.

Too late. The palanquin stopped, a burly guard accompanying the party strode towards him and said, "The Devi wishes to speak with you. Follow me!"

Vikraman followed him. Who is she? Does she recognise me?!

Kuntavi looked at him searchingly, as if to look into his heart and read what she found there. She said, "Sir, who are you? You do not appear to be of this country."

"No, my lady, I am from Shenbaga Islands. I came here to trade in jewels. My name is Devasena," said Vikraman.

Kuntavi must have been surprised but she didn't show it. She sat silent for a minute before saying, "Shenbaga Islands . . . Shenbaga Islands . . . Now where have I heard that before? Who rules there?"

"The line of the earlier kings was wiped out. Vikraman, Prince of the Cholas, rules there now."

The expression on Kuntavi's face changed. His heart leapt. She had not forgotten the exile she had seen! But who was she? So beautiful a face, so commanding a presence. Could she be . . . ? But his mind shied away from the thought.

Then Kuntavi asked, "You are a trader in jewels?"

"Yes, I am. The jewels I have with me are rare and precious. Would you like to see some, Devi?"

"Not here, a crowd will gather. Perhaps you could visit me at the palace in the evening?"

Kuntavi may have been surprised at the odd expression on the young man's face, had she noticed it then. Disappointment and dread were a strange mixture. But she went on, "Yes, come this evening. Princess Kuntavi will be delighted. She loves jewels, even more if they are rare. She might even buy the whole lot from you."

The merchant heaved a sigh. He looked as if a great fear had been removed.

"When you get to the palace gates, ask for Kuntavi's companion Madhavi," said Kuntavi, and added, "You have a huge load of precious stones. Aren't you afraid of robbers?"

"Robbers? In the reign of Narasimha Pallavar?"

Kuntavi smiled. "So! Our emperor's fame has spread that far, has it? Good."

Then, Kuntavi leaned forward and instructed the palanquin bearers to start up again. The merchant stood rooted to the spot, watching the palanquin disappear down the street.

"Well!" said a strangely familiar voice. "How long will you stand there staring? Your eyes will pop out!' The young man jumped as if the street were too hot, and spun around. Leering down at him from astride a horse was Marappa Bhupathi.

Marappan Smiles

Whenever Vikraman had thought of his uncle during his stay in Shenbaga Islands, he had felt only revulsion and a vague astonishment that such a man could be of Chola lineage. The feeling returned.

When Marappan saw Vikraman start and step back, he said mockingly, "Why so worried, young fellow? I heard some talk of thieves. Perhaps you think I am one?"

This gave Vikraman a chance to compose himself. "I have heard that there are no robbers in Narasimha Pallavar's kingdom. So you cannot be a thief."

"What is your name? Where are you from? And why are you here?"

"My name is Devasena. I have come here to trade in jewels."

"Ah! So you trade in jewels, do you? Now why would an honest trader be talking to every other sculptor in such secrecy? Do you know what the penalty is for luring away artists?"

"I don't. I am a foreigner. And who are you?" asked Vikraman.

Marappa Bhupathi laughed harshly. "I am the younger brother of King Parthiban of the Cholas, who died in battle. I am also currently the general, and therefore, leader of the Cholas."

He keenly watched the young man's face, but it remained

impassive. When a few seconds had elapsed, he said, "Perhaps my fame has not spread to the ends of the earth yet. But surely you have heard of the great King Parthiban, bravest of the brave, greatest of the great, the royal one himself?"

The merchant said quietly but with an edge of anger, "I have heard of King Parthiban. His son Vikraman is currently ruler of Shenbaga Islands, where I come from. I am a loyal subject. Do not slight King Parthiban where I can hear you."

The surprise on Marappan's face was genuine. "Such devotion! Such patriotism!" he said mockingly. "It's a privilege to meet one such as this! What is your name again?"

"Devasena."

"Devasena. And what did the princess Kuntavi want with you?"

Vikraman blinked at Marappan. Then the full import of what he had just said struck him. "What are you talking about?" he asked shakily. "She is not the princess's companion, Madhavi?"

"Is that what she told you? She certainly takes after her father," said Marappan. "So, Vikraman is your king? Does he know of the tragedy that befell his mother?"

Vikraman, who had been calm and coolly arrogant all the while, now stared at him, horrified and angry. "What happened? What happened to Arulmozhi Devi?" he asked in a high-pitched voice.

A slow and satisfied smile crept across Marappan's face. The 'merchant' had just committed a fatal error. As they stood frozen facing each other in the street, a huge roar rose up behind them.

"Long live the emperor who vanquished Vatapi! Jaya vijayi bhava!"

And then they heard the next shout go up. "Make way! Make way! The emperor comes! Make way for the emperor!"

Bandits!

The chakravarti was seated on a majestic elephant. He had given no notice of his arrival in Mamallapuram and the people were going crazy with joy, dancing and shouting on the streets as he came.

Marappa Bhupathi slunk away and Vikraman pressed into a thick part of the crowd. He knew he should not see the emperor or he might be recognised. But he wanted to see the emperor. He was a gifted general and peerless warrior, not to mention a just ruler, and Vikraman secretly looked up to him.

Unconsciously, Vikraman's eyes went up towards the emperor's face. At exactly the same moment the emperor was looking over just that section of the crowd where Vikraman was standing. Their eyes met. For a long second, merchant and emperor stared at each other. Then the emperor's gaze went beyond him, not, after all, having lingered. Not even the slightest hesitation, not even a minute lift of the eyebrows. The emperor moved on.

Vikraman heaved a sigh of relief as if he had escaped from a great danger. He stood there until the crowd had dispersed, deep in thought, mainly focused on his disastrous meeting with Marappa Bhupathi. Why had he spoken to him in that manner?

Had he recognised him? Marappan as the Chola senatipati! What a reward for his treachery! And what he said about that woman. Was she really the chakravarti's daughter? If so, why had she lied to him about her identity?

Whichever way he turned, there were dangers. He had to leave Mamallapuram. He also needed to find out what had happened to Arulmozhi Devi. He would have to go to Uraiyur immediately. He had intended to buy a horse to travel to Uraiyur; he now discarded that plan. If he did that, it was very likely that Marappan would be waiting for him. He knew he wouldn't be so lucky and get away a second time. Ironically, though, it had been the emperor who had saved him.

What was his uncle doing here? Why had he come to Mamallapuram? Whatever it was, it was good he was here. While Marappan was in Mamallapuram, he could go quickly to Uraiyur and return. He decided to leave that very night. He hurried towards the chhattram, the common lodging hall he was staying in, to collect the few possessions he had brought along and to get old Chitragupta, who would carry them. He didn't notice Chitragupta signalling secretly to another man standing at the entrance of the building. By the time they set out walking, it was half an hour to sunset, and by the time they left Mamallapuram's outer gates, the sun had turned orange and was dipping beneath the horizon.

The highway between Mamallapuram and Kanchi was always bustling with people. On horseback, on elephant-back, by palanquin, even on foot — people were always travelling to either city or to one of the numerous towns and villages along the route. There were so many temples, sanctuaries and halls or chhattrams one could stay in, places where one could stop for refreshments, shops and stores of all kinds all along the way. A first-time traveller might well wonder if the highway itself was a city.

There were shortcuts, of course, that veered away from the highway at several points to go to various places. One of these was a small road, a path, really, that sliced right through a forest on the way to the highway from Kanchi to Uraiyur. It saved quite some distance. However, it was not much used. There was always the danger of wild animals, and there was also a famous — or infamous — Kali temple hidden somewhere there. Many Saktas or Kapalikas, who belonged to a sect that practised human sacrifice, were rumoured to hang around the Kali temple. Human sacrifice had been outlawed by the emperor, but still, even brave men hesitated to take this path.

Vikraman, however, was unaware of any danger in the path the old man was leading him through. He didn't think there was anything to be afraid of. He needed to get to Uraiyur as soon as possible. That was all. As they made their way, night began closing in. It was winter, and shadows fell across their path. Luckily, the sky was clear and he could see by starlight. The fireflies also put in an appearance, and the night was lit by magic.

But it was also eerie. Even Vikraman, who by no stretch of imagination could be called cowardly, was gradually beginning to feel uneasy. There were strange rustlings in the forest, he could hear animals howling and owls hooting in the distance. Vikraman would have asked how much longer the journey would take, but Chitragupta could not see his gestures in the dark.

Half an hour after darkness had truly closed around them, Vikraman lost all desire to walk any further. His instinct, something he was not likely to disregard, was screaming at him of hidden dangers in the darkness. And then he heard, ever so faintly, a sound very far away — the sound of horses in the forest. He turned to place it correctly and saw the old man listening, head cocked, to catch the sound.

If this man is deaf, how can he . . . Quick as a flash, even before the thought had finished forming, he drew his sword from where it was concealed in his clothes and held it to the false one's throat. The polished, sharpened blade glittered dangerously in the starlight. Vikraman grabbed Chitragupta's hair and said roughly, "Look at me. Tell me the truth. Are you deaf? Can you hear me? If you can, speak up or I'll cut your throat."

Chitragupta raised his face to Vikraman's and cackled evilly. The terrifying sound rose menacingly in the night. Vikraman's blood froze. In the one second that he relaxed his grip, Chitragupta slipped through his hands and ran till he was some ten feet away. Then he opened his mouth wide, cupped his hands around them and screamed. That sound was even worse than his laughter. Not human, not animal, it was something infinitely worse. Anyone who heard it from far away might have thought it was a demon howling in the night.

Vikraman shivered. Still, he controlled himself and ran towards the old man with the intention of killing him. This notion was quickly discarded as trees parted on one side of the path and four men stepped out, making straight for Vikraman. When he saw the long knives in their hands, he actually felt relieved. The night, the solitude, and the man's ghastly laughter, had all combined to frighten him briefly out of his wits. Well, at least now he knew they were not ghosts. Flesh and blood and swords he could handle.

The four of them attacked at once. Since they had surrounded

him, he was forced to spin continually to be able to block all their thrusts. In the first minute, he fatally wounded one of them. He knocked a knife out of one attacker's hands and it fell upon and wounded another who screamed and fell to the ground.

The remaining two realised that he was obviously not an ordinary fighter. They kept their distance, attacking from out of the range of his sword, with the intention of tiring him out. They were succeeding in their efforts.

From the way they kept looking into the forest, he guessed they were expecting someone. The road stretched straight ahead and he saw almost immediately that a man on horseback was approaching. One of the men he was fighting cried out, "Master! Come quickly!"

Vikraman knew he wasn't going to last. He was already tired. He knew he could defeat these two. But with reinforcement, and a fresh opponent on horseback, he knew he could not hold out in his current state. He was sad that he would not see his mother again. He saw, briefly, the woman he had spoken with on the street.

The next picture in his mind was of the scarred face of the Pallava emperor, and he felt regret that a supposedly orderly kingdom like his had banditry and lawlessness. Then he remembered that the same emperor was ruling his beloved country, and the thought gave him enough rage to go on. He efficiently despatched one of the two remaining attackers.

At exactly the same moment, the man on horseback made an incredible throw from the saddle. The knife flashed in the darkness — past Vikraman — and buried itself in the body of the last attacker.

Vikraman was stunned. At first he thought the man had mistaken him for his comrade. But he was the only one wearing an upper garment; the others were bare-chested. It would have been easy to pick him off, especially for someone with the skill this man obviously had. So he was aiming to hit the bandit. Who was he? Certainly not the 'Master' they had been expecting.

The man slid out of the saddle and onto the ground. "Who are you, sir?" he asked of Vikraman. "And what are you doing here?"

The Spymaster

Vikraman felt a surge of gratitude for the stranger. He replied, "I am a merchant. I was travelling to Uraiyur to trade. I came across this path and decided to take it. Thank you for coming to my rescue."

"And do traders wield swords so handily?"

"I trade in jewels. I have, therefore, learned to use weapons . . ."

"A jewel trader, here, at this time of night, alone. It shows a rare lack of discretion!" said the man.

"This was reputed to be a kingdom of law-abiding citizens."

"Aha! A foreigner! I thought as much. Where are you from?"

"Shenbaga Islands."

"I have heard of the Islands. But if you want to trade in jewels, wouldn't Kanchi be the obvious choice?"

Vikraman was dismayed. The man was too sharp. "Who are you who saved my life?"

The man inclined his head, amused. "What does it matter who I am?"

"I would like to know the name of the man who saved my life."

"I didn't save your life, you saved it yourself. Still, since you asked, I am the spymaster of the chakravarti. I heard that you were entering this area alone and came along in case something happened to you."

"Is that so? Well! I had not anticipated such efficiency among the emperor's followers."

"We do our best. And what prevents me from taking you in for murdering four men?"

Vikraman stiffened. His hand went to his sword.

The man saw this and said amiably, "Not that I have that intention, mind you. You are a foreigner and didn't know about this path. If men like you did not exist, sir, we would be looking for work! Goodbye, then," he said and prepared to swing into the saddle.

Vikraman wondered what to do. He felt he had not thanked the spymaster properly. He wondered whether he could buy the horse the man rode. He needed a place to sleep.

"No," he said quietly. "If you had not come, I might have lost my life today. I must get to Uraiyur. But I cannot walk through this forest at night."

"I see. You want my horse. But even if I gave it to you, you would not survive the night. I know a place where we can get food and rest. Continue your journey in the morning."

Vikraman weighed his options. "All right," he said.

The man casually lifted the heavy sack of jewels and tied it to the horse. Then, without a backward glance, he walked off with long strides down the path. Both weary and wary, Vikraman followed behind.

The Sculptor's House

There was a side trail that cut sharply off from the main path. It seemed it was a gloomy enough sight during the day; it was depressing at night. Even the faint starlight was blocked out by sneaking creepers. Down such a trail Vikraman walked, dead tired, following a man he had not known until that night — whom he still didn't really know. The man could have been anybody. Vikraman's heart beat faster than it should. Creepers and branches brushed irritatingly against him. Owls hooted and shrieked jarringly.

A deep roar sounded from a far section of the forest. The horse whickered and jumped a little. The man stroked it with disconcerting gentleness, as if to say, "Do not fear, I am with you." It was a strange procession — the horse, followed by the spymaster, with Vikraman bringing up the rear.

At one point, Vikraman stumbled and fell. The spymaster reached, caught his wrist and steadied him without the least apparent effort. Vikraman was shocked by the strength the man so casually displayed. This man was certainly no ordinary man. He was almost certainly a high-ranking soldier. Gods, but that chakravarti picked the perfect men for each job!

When he was about to ask whether they would have to walk

much farther, Vikraman found that they were in a clearing and the stars were glittering overhead. In that distant light, Vikraman could just about make out the outlines of a building. "We can spend the night here. You can leave at dawn," said the spymaster.

"But who built this house? In this kind of place at that? Why?" asked Vikraman.

"The man who built this house is not here any more. When he lived here, the forest was not such a dark and thick place. It is a long story, I shall tell it to you later if you do not wish to sleep," replied the man.

The spymaster rapped on the door. The door opened. There was an old woman inside holding a lamp in her hands. When she saw the spymaster, her eyes widened in shock. Cleverly blocking Vikraman's view, the spymaster put a finger on his lips. The woman's face cleared of all emotion. "Come in, sir," she said calmly and held the door wide open.

When they went in, the horse walked past them, past the veranda to a side door, as if accustomed to the place. The old woman opened the door and it went through.

The spymaster turned to Vikraman with a smile. "Isn't that horse quick? When I was here last time, I put it there and now it goes by itself. I must go and see to it. Enjoy the sculptures." And he disappeared. The woman followed him.

Vikraman veered around slowly. He saw that the room was full of sculptures and drawings, mostly of a girl. Obviously the sculptor was a genius. The girl's stunning beauty and the love of the creator were apparent in the strokes that made her figure in stone and in paint. Most of the sculptures and drawings depicted her in dance poses, with different expressions on her delicately chiselled face. Vikraman was moved. The paintings and sculptures displayed in Uraiyur or Mamallapuram were nothing compared to the loveliness that lay within this ramshackle building.

The spymaster entered, presumably having seen to his horse's feed. Vikraman turned to him with wonder in his eyes. "Who did these?" he asked. "They are beautiful! And why have they been left here, in the middle of nowhere, when in fact the people of all nations should see them."

"As I said before," replied the spymaster, "it is a long story. If you want to spend the night listening, I will be happy to tell you. But first I intend to eat. The lady will serve us food." They sat down to eat.

Vikraman asked, "What is your name? You have not told me."

"My name is Virasena. And yours?"

"Devasena," said Vikraman, surprised.

"Good, our names gives us a bond. Tell me, why were you going to Uraiyur?" Suspicion coloured Vikraman's view of the man again. *If he finds out . . . I must be careful.*

"My mother lives in Uraiyur. I wanted to go quickly to visit her." He was deliberately vague.

"You said you belonged to Shenbaga Islands!"

"I was born and brought up here. I went to the Islands to earn money when the Pallavas took over. What jewel trade is worth it in a kingdom without royalty?"

He hoped maybe Virasena would rise to his subtle bait about the royal family and reveal what had happened to his mother, but no, he remained silent until the end of the meal. When they had finished, he asked Virasena again about the story of the house they were in.

"In this house, thirty years ago," he said, "lived Ayana the sculptor and his daughter Sivakami." It seemed as if Virasena

was talking more to himself now, reflectively. "The house was filled with the sound of anklets. Sivakami was a dancer, a divine dancer. Her father drew his inspiration from her. He would watch her dance and then he would draw and sculpt her."

"So she was the one?" said Vikraman, struck by the passion in the other man's voice.

"Yes, she was the one. I used to come here a lot, you know. It was the time of Mahendra Varman, his son must have been as old as you are now. I would come with him — Narasimha Varman. Even from afar, we could hear the two of them in the house — anklet and chisel, the sound would greet us. I cannot believe they are gone, that their spirits are gone. I think they are still here, unquiet spirits. Listen. Can't you hear the chisel strike stone? The tinkle of the anklets?"

Vikraman begged Virasena to tell him the rest of the story. Virasena talked about the great love that Narasimha Varman had for Sivakami when he was prince. Then came Pulikesi's invasion from the north, and Sivakami's capture. Narasimhan's grief, his father's death, and Sivakami's oath not to return to her homeland until Vatapi was reduced to ashes by Narasimhan. The battle to free Sivakami and the killing of Pulikesi. And then, although the oath had been fulfilled, the terms laid upon her lover satisfied, the terrible realisation that their love would never be fulfilled, and in heartbreak and sorrow the tale closed.

Vikraman had tears running down his face. The admiration he had for the emperor, unacknowledged even to himself, now came into the open and he found that it had grown into a kind of love. He saw that all the anger and hate he had had towards him had dissipated. He could never think of him as an enemy again. But he would have to. Remembering his promise to his father helped.

When the story was over, dawn was breaking and birds were singing in the trees. Vikraman and Virasena lay back and slept for about half an hour. When Vikraman awoke to sunshine, he wondered briefly whether the events of the previous night had been a dream. Then he turned his head and saw the dazzling sculptures.

A cheery voice called from outside, "Devasena! Your horse is ready, fed and rested, having had a good night's sleep, unlike us." After he had bathed and eaten the meagre food the old woman provided, Vikraman took leave of Virasena. "I am greatly indebted to you. You saved my life, and now you give me this horse. I refuse to go without paying for it. You must take these gems in return." And he took a handful and gave it to the spymaster.

"Wrong again. This horse is a loan. When your business in Uraiyur is done, leave this horse here."

"All right, but I will give you these gems as a gift." Virasena accepted the gift.

Vikraman got on the horse. The spymaster patted its nose and said, "This horse knows the way to Uraiyur. If you allow it to, it will take you there by the shortest route."

The horse set off down the road. Vikraman kept looking back at the ruined house inside which lay such a precious treasure until it disappeared from sight. And at the man — well-built, majestic, with a strange light on his face that seemed to come from a great store of it within — until he too disappeared from view.

Scattered Jewels

The spymaster waited until Vikraman was out of sight before going back into the house. He stood for a long time before the sculpture of the girl. There seemed to be a deep sorrow etched on his face. Then he sought out the old woman and said, "This boy might return in a while. Give him shelter and food, but for God's sake don't let him know my secret! I shall return in six days."

He brought out a horse from the stable, similar to the one Vikraman had ridden away upon. Lightly he jumped upon it and rode in the opposite direction, towards the site of the ambush. He soon reached it.

That was when he got his first surprise. He gazed upon the area with a practised eye, but he saw nothing! He had expected to see a gory sight since wild animals would certainly have found the corpses at night. But there was no sign of any such thing. No sign of corpses, much less half-eaten corpses. Someone had dragged them away! But who?

He commenced a closer inspection. A glint of white caught his eye. It was a human skull! Old and stained with age. It did not belong to any of the men killed the night before. Whoever had come here to dispose of the bodies was a Kapalika, deduced the spymaster. Then something else made him snap his head around

— there were some gems lying on the ground. They must have dropped out of a loosely-tied pack when the old man let the sack fall in the scuffle. In the hurry to leave the place, he had not noticed it. The spymaster stooped to pick them up.

Then he heard hoofbeats. He jumped back onto his horse, rode it away from the road and left it there before walking back to where he could clearly see and hear everything without being seen himself. Presently six horsemen came into view.

When the spymaster caught a glimpse of the leader's face, his jaw tightened with dislike. The leader of the group was Marappa Bhupathi. Marappan roughly reined his horse to a stop. His men formed a rough circle around him. Marappan made a cursory inspection of the area and when he found the jewels, he laughed harshly. "Looks like we've saved ourselves some work," he remarked cryptically. Then they all moved off down the road at a gallop.

When he was sure they were gone, the spymaster rode off towards the highway. Some distance away, he got a foul stench from behind a rock where vultures were feeding upon carcasses. Obviously, Vikraman's attackers had been found.

Not lingering any longer, the spymaster made off onto the rajapattai just a little ahead of a royal procession. His keen eyes saw a palanquin and a stallion and the Lion flag. The Pallava prince and princess! He did not slow down. Instead, he touched his heels to the horse and it sped down the road with its rider bent low over its body. They were headed for Kanchi.

Impostor!

The spymaster's sudden, deliberate flight ahead of the procession heading towards Kanchi did not go unnoticed by either Kuntavi or Mahendran. Mahendran was as remarkable as Kuntavi and their father. He had his sister's colouring and features and her softness, combined with his father's air of command, valour and majesty. Mahendran had been ruling on behalf of his father for one year. Therefore, it was surprising the man had not slowed to pay respects and follow the royal procession, as was the custom.

"Do you see that man over there? The one in front, riding away? He looks like a soldier. Would you know him?" Kuntavi asked her brother from her palanquin.

"No," said Mahendran shading his eyes with a hand and looking down the road. "Well-built. And what a horse!" He was riding on a horse alongside the palanquin.

"Looks like he's going to Kanchi," commented Kuntavi. "Must be a foreigner. Or else, why didn't he stop? There was a ship that docked four days ago which had foreigners on it. May be one of them."

"Did that jewel trader come to the palace?" asked Mahendran. "Oh, well, he may come to Kanchi."

Kuntavi didn't reply. If her suspicions were accurate, he most certainly would not come to the Kanchi court. She compared the man she had seen in Kanchi three years ago and the one she had met in Mamallapuram yesterday. The resemblance was too great to be a simple coincidence. Mahendran picked up the signals her silence conveyed. "Sister," he said. "I have reached a decision. I intend to undertake a sea voyage soon."

"To Lanka?" asked Kuntavi.

"No, to Shenbaga Islands."

"Why?" asked Kuntavi, instantly alert.

"I intend to ask Father to forgive Vikraman. When he does, I shall personally go to the Islands and bring him back here. Sister, I haven't seen you really happy in all the year I've been here. I want to see you happy, Kuntavi." He saw Kuntavi avert her face, but he knew she was crying. Then she looked up.

"Father will never agree."

"I will make him. I wanted to ask him yesterday, but he was not there. I will do it tonight."

"What is the use of Father forgiving him?"

"What use? I will have a brother-in-law!"

"Oh, go on!" said Kuntavi.

"I'll go all right, all the way to Shenbaga Islands. And if I don't find that prince, tie him up in a sack, and bring him back here to you, my name isn't Mahendran, and that's a promise!"

When Kuntavi and Mahendran arrived in Kanchi, they parted ways to go to their own sections of the palace. When Kuntavi entered her rooms in the women's wing, she was shocked to see a strange man seated upon the chair reserved for her father. She asked furiously, "Who are you? How dare you enter these apartments!"

"Devi, I am the spymaster of the Pallava Empire. My name is Virasena. I came to visit you about righting a wrong."

Kuntavi's anger faded away. Happiness and a trace of embarrassment replaced it. "Father? What are you – what have you done to yourself?" And she ran to her father and pulled off the false moustache, revealing the smiling, clean-shaven face of the Pallava emperor. "It was only the voice, or I wouldn't have found out. Where did you learn this?" she asked.

The chakravarti's eyes twinkled. "From my father," he replied.

Cause and Effect

Kuntavi stared at her father, astonished. "Why would my grandfather teach you this? Surely disguises are only for actors?"

"I consider it the most useful thing he ever taught me," said the emperor. "There are many arts a king must know, and this is very important. Thanks to this, I get to know my subjects' honest opinions and problems, learn my enemy's secret weakness, if I must punish a crime . . ."

Kuntavi cut in. "And do you suspect me of one of those crimes?" she laughed, displaying a perfect set of teeth.

"I don't suspect, I know. You, my dear daughter, are personally responsible for the deaths of four men last night. Did you invite a foreign merchant to the palace, claiming to be the princess's companion Madhavi?"

"Yes, is that a crime?" Kuntavi was defensive.

"That was the cause of the whole thing. This unfortunate man thought he was in some great danger because someone must have told him who you were. Therefore, he took off for Uraiyur."

"Why did he go there instead of to Kanchi? I mean, it's not like he would have any real business there, because there wouldn't be any opportunities for him."

"His mother lives in Uraiyur, and he went to visit her,"

replied her father. Kuntavi's suspicions as to the identity of the merchant were strengthened. Her thoughts went back to the Chola prince. "He was attacked by four men when he was travelling by an unsafe short-cut," continued her father. "But this young man is more than he seems to be. He finished off three of them before I got there and killed the last one."

"What of the legend of perfect peace in Narasimha Varman's reign? If thieves can operate so close to Kanchi and Mamallapuram, well . . . !" said Kuntavi.

"I was thinking along the same lines. But then I discovered they were Kapalikas."

"Oh!" cried Kuntavi, shocked. "Do they still plague our land? I thought you had abolished the practice!"

"No, such barbarism still exists. I can only hunt it down, but stupidity and blind belief I cannot eradicate. If I destroy it here, it springs up somewhere else," said the emperor.

"That poor trader!" said Kuntavi. "He was in so much danger! Lucky you were there!"

"Oh, he is a thief too, or else he would not have fled Mamallapuram in such a hurry. He tried to lure some of my best artisans over to his island. The man he hired to carry his goods was a pawn of the Kapalikas. He led the merchant down a pre-arranged route and had him waylaid. If I hadn't arrived when I did . . ."

"So what happened after that?" asked Kuntavi, eagerly.

The emperor related what had happened and added that he had sent Vikraman to Uraiyur on his own horse. Kuntavi asked whether the man had guessed her father's identity. "No, why?" he retorted.

She was silent for a second and then she said, "I just wanted to know how well the disguise worked."

"Oh, Marappa Bhupathi was in Mamallapuram yesterday," said the emperor. "Can you tell me why?"

"Mahendran and I invited him," she said. "Achyuta Varman sent a message from Uraiyur that he felt he was getting too old to be managing the Chola kingdom. So my brother agreed to install Marappa Bhupathi instead."

"Ah!" said the Emperor. Kuntavi picked up her veena and began to play.

The Flood

In the time of Mahendra Pallavar and Narasimha Varman, the Shaiva and Vaishnava sects of Hinduism were being rejuvenated. They had also embraced some of the philosophies of the Jain and Buddhist religions. Some of the greatest Tamil poets and devotees lived at the time — Appar, Sundarar, Jnana Sambandar. It was the golden age of religious art in the southern region.

At the same time, violent sects such as the Kapalikas, the Saktas and the Bhairavas also secretly flourished. Unbelievable and distressing as it may sound, human sacrifice was rampant among members of these sects. Sometimes they cut off their own heads at sacrificial ceremonies in the hope that it would bring them great benefits in the next life.

It was believed that Pulikesi of Vatapi had brought these sects with him when he had marched upon the fertile Pallava lands. After the invasion, severe famine seized the land and in that time of trouble, people turned to these cannibalistic religious sects for succour.

Narasimha Varman had tried his utmost to abolish these sects. When he realised that outlawing such practices made no difference — for who could threaten a man willing to cut his own throat? — he entrusted the administration of his empire to his son and was currently roaming the land in disguise, investigating the cults.

Vikraman, though, was unaware of any danger other than having been robbed as he travelled to Uraiyur. He did not need to ask directions. Just like the spymaster had said, the horse knew the way well.

As Vikraman passed through a forest in the early evening, he felt the air grow chill. He looked up and saw a black curtain of clouds in the east, hastening towards him. Dead leaves stirred and circled in the restless breeze that intensified and cooled with every moment. It carried the scent of rain. As he quickened his pace, the clouds finally wiped the sun out and the skies opened up. It was a manifestation of pure power — hard, swift, cold, stinging, destructive. The rain poured upon the ground. Shivering from the wet and the cold, Vikraman rode faster to reach shelter.

When he had gone a short distance, he found his way obstructed by a river. In this rain, and with the wind on its back, it was dangerously full and could flood at any moment. Vikraman judged his options and then decided he would be safer if he crossed the river before it flooded and blocked his way for days. As he led the horse into the water, Vikraman felt it being pushed off its feet. It began swimming desperately. Knowing they would both die if he stayed on its back, Vikraman swung himself free and dived into the swirling waters.

A Familiar Voice

The rough waters tossed him around. Gasping, Vikraman struck out with all his might. He swam desperately for a mudbank in the middle of the river and pulled himself onto it. Both banks were approximately the same distance from where he lay. He slid back into the river, angling downstream and aiming to reach a huge banyan tree that was faintly visible.

Vikraman saw his horse struggling up the bank. *Well, at least it's going to make it,* he thought, and knew a moment's bleak relief. His arms were tiring. The water had risen in speed and force — enough, he thought, to sweep away an elephant. He knew it would succeed in sweeping him away.

Alas for fate! So much for hopes, for castles in the air. Father died on the battlefield. But I? An ignominious death in a forest flood, of all things! Was this the reason for coming back home — to die?! Without seeing my mother? Without her knowing that I had been King of a free land, vassal to none, however briefly. If I had only had the chance to seek out the woman in Mamallapuram, whoever she is, and ask her to marry me. And the man who saved my life, I will never see him again . . .

Vikraman was finished. He knew it, accepted it. Enough. His eyes closed, his mind grew dull.

And then, suddenly, there came to his mind an image of swimming in the Kaveri. He had nearly drowned, exhausted from battling the river, and Ponnan, laughing, had picked him up easily in his arms and swum to the shore. *Ah, Ponna, where are you?* He slipped, tired, oh, so tired, into the night.

He heard a voice calling him as if from a great distance, "Maharaja!" Who? Someone he knew. Ponnan? Vikraman wondered whether he was dreaming, unconscious, or dead. He was just about to regretfully decide on the last, when he found he hadn't opened his eyes yet. He did so and was shocked. It was Ponnan.

He was soaking wet, his hair was plastered to his head, tears and water were streaming down his face.

"Ponna!" Vikraman said hoarsely. "Is it really you?"

They were both on the shore, Vikraman's head in Ponnan's lap. The rain had stopped. A light scent of earth wafted upon a gentle breeze. It was twilight. Vikraman snapped upright.

"Do you know? Just as I was about to drown I was thinking

of you. Swimming in the Kaveri when you were always there to pull me out if I went under. When I saw someone at the shore, I thought for one instant, was it you? And then I fainted. It was you! How? How could it be?"

"Well, I was watching the flood from a safe distance, and I saw someone on a horse. I didn't know it was you, of course. I saw you try to swim for the shore. I saw you go under. I almost didn't come. If I hadn't . . . Oh!" Ponnan covered his eyes.

"Why think about that now?" said Vikraman gently. "You did save me, by the grace of the Lord, and the aid of my father watching over me. But forget that whole business. How is the queen?"

Ponnan's eyes filled with tears. Vikraman, terrified, clutched his shoulder. "What happened?" he demanded harshly, concealing his fear. "What happened to her? Tell me! Is she – is she – dead?"

"No," said Ponnan. "She isn't dead and that is all we know for sure."

The Solar Eclipse

Night had well and truly closed in by the time they sat under the roof of a wayside shelter, the Mahendra Mandapam. Then Ponnan began to tell his story — about Arulmozhi's loneliness, and how she had finally left on a pilgrimage with Paranjyoti Adigal.

In the Thai month of the previous year, they had been in Paranjyoti Adigal's hometown, Tiruchengattangudi. It was the day of total solar eclipse. They had decided to bathe in the sea, at the holy confluence at the delta of the Kaveri. People had come from all over. Ponnan and Valli were there too. Arulmozhi, the siruthondar, his wife, and Ponnan and Valli all went to bathe together. The silt deposited by the Kaveri made the sea incredibly shallow for a long stretch. The eclipse commenced. The sun dimmed. The sea seemed to rise.

To see the sun go out in the middle of the day sent a sudden, irrational spasm of fear among the people. The devout were lost in ecstasy. Arulmozhi, eyes closed, hands clasped, was facing east, praying silently.

Valli had never seen the sea before. Her heart was pounding, even though Ponnan had one arm around her, holding her securely. As she was about to get out of the water, the queen opened her eyes and exclaimed, "Vikrama! My son! I'm coming!" Her voice rose above the sound of the waves and the people and she ran straight into the sea.

Ponnan and Valli screamed. The siruthondar opened his eyes and looked up, saying, "What? What happened?"

"The queen has jumped into the water!" shouted Ponnan.

And in that moment, when they needed it the most, the sun disappeared entirely.

The Kapala Bhairavar

When he heard that his mother had cried out for him, Vikraman's eyes filled with tears. "How did you find her?" he asked.

"She's definitely alive. What we don't know is where she is. We just couldn't find her. Now that you're here . . ." And Ponnan went on with his story.

Ponnan and the siruthondar searched as long as they could. There was no sign of her. Finally, the siruthondar said sorrowfully, "Leave it, Ponna. The sea has taken her." At this Ponnan started to cry.

When they went back to their wives, the women said excitedly that they had seen a one-armed man carrying a woman and that the woman had looked very much like Arulmozhi Devi. But even as they had called out, he had vanished into the crowd.

Ponnan and the siruthondar began searching for the man. But they found neither the man nor his captive. After a long, tiring and worthless search, they wondered whether Valli and the siruthondar's wife had dreamt the whole thing. But the women swore upon what they had seen.

When the Shivanadiyar visited them at Uraiyur, he said, "I believe Valli completely. Queen Arulmozhi has been kidnapped. The question is, where is she? She must have been taken by the Kapala Rudra Bhairavar, head priest of the Kapalikas in this region. He has been causing a lot of trouble and I want to find him and the headquarters of his sect. The queen must be in his hideout."

Ponnan was horrified. "If he sacrifices her . . ."

"No, I don't think he will." The Shivanadiyar sounded confident. "There is some other reason for his activities."

They decided to split up to search for the Kapala Rudra Bhairavar, with Ponnan combing the Chola region, and the Shivanadiyar the Pallava realm. Ponnan left Valli at his aunt's, and began his pursuit of the Kapalikas.

He had come to a mountain, forbiddingly covered with thorn trees and creepers. The mountain had broken away slightly from the Kolli hills. Judging by the thickness of its natural vegetation, which would deter anyone who wanted to climb the mountain, Ponnan deduced that this would be exactly where he would have placed a Kali temple that he didn't want discovered. He had also heard tell of savage sects living in these forests. He had heard rumours that they even engaged in human sacrifice.

So he began looking for a way into the thick growth. When he had climbed from morning to afternoon, he finally collapsed on top of a rock. He had wanted to climb down to the nearest village by night, not having any pressing desire to be eaten by whatever animals inhabited the place. That's when he had heard voices. He had barely enough time to hide when he saw two men coming down the hill, if the creatures that were walking towards him could be called men.

One was certainly a man. The factors that led to this deduction were his savage, rolling, bloodshot eyes, his tall and broad body, his long, thick, fiercely curling moustache, and matted, unkempt thick hair that came down a cruel face to his shoulders. Blood-red vermilion smeared on his forehead completed the picture. He wore a dark, ash-coloured blanket about his upper body. When he leapt from one rock to another, Ponnan screamed. Or rather, he would have if his throat hadn't been clogged with fear. When the blanket slipped from his shoulder, Ponnan saw that he had only one arm.

So this was the man who had carried away Arulmozhi! This was the Kapala Bhairavar.

If the Kapala Bhairavar was terrifying, the person who accompanied him was worse. As they came closer, Ponnan saw that it was indeed a man, only about as tall as a ten-year-old with the dried up face of a very old person and hair all over his face. He jumped nimbly from rock to rock on his way down. His very sight sent shivers down Ponnan's spine.

Vikraman interrupted Ponnan's narration and made him describe the old man accurately. Then Ponnan asked, "Why? Did you meet someone like that on your way?"

"Yes – I'll tell you later about that. Go on."

"Oh, there isn't much after that! I followed the stream while I could. Then I came to a waterfall. I swear to you, there was no way I could have scaled it. There must have been a secret way, because to come down was as impossible as climbing up. I finally thought I would inform the Shivanadiyar of this, and came back down the river. And thank God for it," he said fervently, finishing his story.

"Yes, thank God, or else I might have been greeting my forefathers at this moment. My mother will not die before seeing me again. She calls me when I sleep, she is calling me this minute. Oh, Mother, Mother!" Vikraman was nearly shrieking.

Ponnan clamped an authoritative hand over Vikraman's mouth. "Quiet, Maharaja!" he said. 'Listen! Someone comes!'

In the darkness, they saw faintly that two men were talking. They were right outside the place where Ponnan and Vikraman had taken shelter.

Kali's Thirst

Ponnan inched to the doorway and peered out. He strained to make out who they were. Then lightning flared gloriously in the sky. Ponnan started. One was Marappa Bhupathi. The other was the Kapala Bhairavar. When Vikraman placed Marappan's voice, he went for the door and it took all Ponnan's strength to drag him back.

"Great lord! What else has Mother Kali in mind for me? Tell this humble servant, that he may carry out her orders!" said Marappa.

A harsh voice replied, "The Mother has many great things in store for you, many privileges. She also expects more from you. She thirsts! I await one whose blood goes back centuries.

I knew he was coming. Last month, the Mother spoke. Through Queen Arulmozhi her voice came. 'The ship is setting out! He comes!' she cried. I had laid a trap for him! And you, you fool, sidetracked him!"

"Great Lord, I beg forgiveness!"

"The Mother has forgiven you. But she cries for blood to slake her thirst! Next month, we must have the ceremony. If you bring the prince . . ."

"If I bring the prince?"

". . . the Mother holds the crown of the Cholas."

"Only that?"

"Oh, she has much more!"

"Such as?"

"She is ready to give you the throne of the Pallavas!"

"Ahhhhh," said Marappan. There was silence for a while.

"But it will not come unearned. Bring me the son of Parthiban!"

"I will. And then?"

"Offer her your head!"

Marappan shrieked.

"If you do, you shall be emperor in your next birth. Or else . . ."

"What?"

"Or else another fitting sacrifice. The Shivanadiyar — you know which one I speak of."

"Great lord! If the blood of ancient kings is insufficient, what good is that of a Shivanadiyar?"

"That is a great secret, a true mystery. Come close, and let me tell it in your ear . . ."

The eavesdroppers strained their ears. But they could hear nothing. Then Marappan laughed gratingly.

"Why do you laugh? Have you no faith in me?" demanded the Bhairava angrily.

"I believe you, great lord. But I am already under orders to capture him. By the emperor's daughter, Kuntavi Devi!"

The sound of hoofbeats cut short the conversation. Six or seven men on horseback, all carrying torches, came along. *All right, we're dead*, thought Ponnan. His heart pounded loudly. He pulled his head back inside.

"Great lord, my men approach. I must leave," said Marappan.

"We shall meet at the usual place. Chitragupta will await you," came the reply. Then there was silence.

Ponnan sighed. "What did we escape from?" he inquired rhetorically.

"Do you know?" said Vikraman ruefully. "Not only did I leave that horse behind when I jumped into that river, and all my jewels, I even managed to drop my sword! Now what do I do?"

"When the queen left on her pilgrimage, she entrusted a box to me . . ."

"What box?"

'It holds the sword your ancestors wore, the one with jewels in the hilt . . ."

"When my father left for battle, he showed me the box and said, 'This is all the heritage I can give you, and all you will need.' This was the sword, Ponna, that belonged to Karikal Valavan! Have you kept it safe?"

"It's in the summer palace. Where else?" said Ponnan.

"All right, we head for Vasanta Maaligai. My father said, 'Vikrama! As long as you are paying taxes to another king, do not even touch this sword. The day you become king of even a field-sized but free kingdom, that day, my son, you will earn the right to wear this sword, and wear it with pride.' I am ruler of a free Shenbaga Islands. I can wear the sword now. That was why I came back."

"Not only Shenbaga Islands, but of the Chola land as well," said Ponnan.

"Not yet. It is not time for that. But it will be soon, very soon, I promise."

They decided to get the sword, find the Shivanadiyar and seek his assistance in rescuing the queen. They resolved to leave for Uraiyur the next morning. What neither of them took into account was the fact that Vikraman would shortly be running a raging fever and he would be in no state to move out of the shelter, much less travel to Uraiyur.

The Horse Returns

Kuntavi's father was everything to her — father and mother, teacher and friend, all rolled in one. She went to him with all her concerns, important or trivial. For a long time they had been together, two bodies and one soul, father and daughter. But now there was a veil between them. The cause was the young prince who had been exiled. She had not forgotten him. No matter how hard she tried. She wanted to talk about him. But how could she?

Every time she brought up the subject, her father pretended he didn't understand and made some innocuous comment. For the first time in her life, Kuntavi wished she had a mother.

She had attempted to befriend Arulmozhi Devi but she had left on her pilgrimage that very day. They had spent a few days together at Mamallapuram once, when the Devi had visited. But for Arulmozhi, Kuntavi was the daughter of the man who had exiled her only son.

Kuntavi, on the other hand, did not believe that her father had given a less than just verdict. Her love of her father was matched only by her pride in him. To live under such a chakravarti, she felt, was itself honour for a petty king. When the Cholas had been paying taxes to the Pallavas for two hundred years, what was the problem in doing so now? Their ideas and ideals were completely different, and therefore the relationship between Kuntavi and Arulmozhi was an uneasy one as they circled around the topics closest to them, like fencers in a duel.

One day, Arulmozhi had opened up somewhat. She told Kuntavi about how her marriage came to be and how, when Vikraman was a young boy, she had dreamt of marrying him to Kuntavi. When she said that, Kuntavi's heart yearned for her to say the thing she wanted her to. Then Arulmozhi said, "But all that ended as a dream! Marry some luckier prince, my child, and live happily."

Kuntavi retorted: "Thank you, no. I have no desire to marry just any prince. I intend to give up the world and become a Shivabhakta!" Arulmozhi, however, didn't understand the implications of that statement.

Another time, Kuntavi casually mentioned that if Vikraman were to agree not to revolt and to pay taxes, he might yet be forgiven. This time, it was Arulmozhi who flared up: "I would rather welcome the news that he is dead!"

The Shivanadiyar had visited Arulmozhi once while she was in Mamallapuram, and Kuntavi nearly bumped into him as she went in to see the queen. They stared at each other in surprise. Then he hurried off.

She went in and asked Arulmozhi who he was. Arulmozhi was unable to provide a name but said that he was revered by her family as their ancestral god after her husband's death. *Ancestral god or ancestral devil?* thought Kuntavi, but kept her mouth shut. Later, when she heard of the episode of Arulmozhi's disappearance, she privately reflected that he must have carried her off for some dark purpose of his own.

A while before this incident occurred, Mahendran, her

brother, had come up from Lanka. She was able to talk to him a little. When Mahendran heard the whole story, he expressed his desire to go to sea once more and bring Vikraman back under some pretext. The emperor flatly refused this request saying that he himself was intending to undertake a sea voyage, and Mahendran would have to stay back and attend to his duties as heir. There was no way Mahendran could disregard a direct order.

Kuntavi had intervened to make Marappan the general of the Chola region. He was given orders to capture the Shivanadiyar, elicit imformation as to Arulmozhi's location, and hand the Shivanadiyar over to Kuntavi. He was also instructed to make the summer palace ready for Kuntavi and Mahendran, in case they should visit.

On the afternoon of the day after Vikraman was trapped in the flood, Kuntavi and Mahendran were on the rajapattai approximately a kada away from the river. Kuntavi was in her palanquin and Mahendran, as usual, was on a horse, riding beside her. He was telling her of his travels in Lanka and the wars he had fought. At times, though, her mind went back to the handsome merchant she had met. She felt mildly surprised. She didn't know what her mind was trying to tell her.

No, no, it's just an extreme resemblance, she convinced herself. *If it had really been him, Father would have noticed.* And so on and so forth. She absently hummed and hahhed at what her brother was saying. And then she saw something that made her sit up very straight.

It was a white horse, riderless. It seemed . . . familiar. And then it came nearer. Her suspicions were proved right. It was her father's. Was Father . . . ? No, she had bid him farewell in Kanchi and there was no way he could have come this far ahead, and why would he leave his horse so carelessly . . . ? Then she remembered that he had given a horse to the jewel merchant. So this was that horse. But where was the merchant?

Kuntavi's stomach churned and her breath stopped in her throat.

On the Riverbank

Mahendran saw his sister's face grow pale. She suddenly looked ill. "What is it?" he asked urgently.

A shaking hand lifted to point out the horse. She seemed incapable of speech.

"Well. It's only a horse, silly, not a lion or a tiger. Why are you so scared?"

Speech returned. "It's Father's horse, Pushpakam!"

"What! What is it doing here? We left Father in Kanchi!" said Mahendran.

"He gave one of his horses to the merchant from Shenbaga Islands."

"Ah!"

The horse was very close now. At a quiet order from Mahendran, a soldier caught it and led it to Kuntavi. She spoke softly to it and stroked its back. It arched its head with pleasure and whinnied. They took it along. Anxiously, Kuntavi asked her brother, "What do you think happened to the merchant?"

Mahendran said carelessly, "Who knows? A horse which was the mount of the Pallava chakravarti might have resented his ways and thrown him somewhere!" He laughed, not realising the disastrous impact his words might have had on his sister.

Kuntavi was in a bad state, no doubt. But one small piece of logic lurked in her mind. If a horse could throw the man, he was most certainly not the Chola prince. The chakravarti had spoken of his valour and . . .

As they travelled on, she noticed that the road they were on was wet and dark. The trees were glistening, and the wind was cold. "Must have rained a lot last night," said Mahendran cheerily. "Not that a drop fell in Kanchi, of course!"

Kuntavi's agile mind leaped far ahead. There had been a storm, the river had flooded, the merchant . . . Was he dead? Would they find his lifeless body? She shuddered. When they reached the river, it was quiet. But debris from the flood was stuck in the lower branches of the trees. Such floods, she knew, were swift to rise and quick to settle. She now knew most of what had happened. He had gone into the river, not expecting the flood. The horse had made it to the bank, waited for him, and then given up and left. The young man had probably died.

The procession began to cross the ford. But Pushpakam sprang back. When its feet touched the water, it reared up, terrified, broke loose from the man holding its reins, spun around, and darted past the procession, straight towards Kanchi.

"Well, the name was rightly kept. It does show a turn of speed, doesn't it?" asked Mahendran of no one in particular.

A Feeble Voice

The party stopped to eat on the banks of the river. Many different kinds of food were placed in front of Kuntavi and Mahendran. The prince ate heartily but Kuntavi ate nothing. Her mind was absorbed with the merchant's death. Was it not said that the souls of those who had died an untimely death roamed the place of their demise for many years? She shuddered. Would one find, if one looked long enough, the ghost of the jewel merchant, wandering the river at night?

She then heard, faintly, a voice calling out. What was it saying? "Mother! Mother!" called the voice. Kuntavi shivered. She said to her brother, "There seems to be someone calling out somewhere. Can you hear it?"

"Yes, someone's calling 'Mother, Mother'. But where is the voice coming from?"

"Probably that shelter there." Kuntavi directed her palanquin to the shelter. *There is some mystery here that will be sorted out now, some secret revealed,* she thought breathlessly, as it became clear that the voice was indeed emanating from there.

The voice was Vikraman's.

Ponnan and Vikraman had left early in the morning, but they hadn't gone ten paces before Vikraman collapsed in a heap, his legs quite unable to do a task as complex as keeping him upright. Ponnan laid Vikraman on a rough bed of grass and hay. The fever was getting worse. Ponnan hadn't eaten in days. If he collapsed as well, it would do no good. Reluctantly, he asked Vikraman's permission to go and fetch a physician. Vikraman weakly assented but after Ponnan left, he had slipped into a delirium. All he could do was moan, "Mother! Mother!" over and over.

It was in this state that Kuntavi found him. Her palanquin stopped outside the mandapam. Kuntavi stood for a second right outside the inner building, looking in. It was the jewel merchant, all right, and he looked as if he was seriously ill. His wide eyes stared up at her for a moment, and then he closed them and began crying out softly again. She called out sharply to her brother, asking him to come over immediately. Their physician made a quick diagnosis. He said it was a high fever that would take ten days to subside.

Thereafter, events moved swiftly. The physician spread a strange concoction on Vikraman's tongue. Then they lifted him up and placed him in Kuntavi's palanquin. Kuntavi was a good rider, so she was on horseback. The procession continued down the road.

Ponnan, meanwhile, had had to search quite far to find a physician. When he finally returned with one, and a cart in which to carry Vikraman, he discovered that he had vanished! Ponnan felt as if someone had kicked him very hard in the stomach.

Parantakam

Ponnan searched the empty mandapam several times. He briefly entertained the notion that everything that he had been through since the previous night had been a dream. As if everything else wasn't bad enough, the physician and the cartman began getting restless. He finally paid them a gold coin from his emergency money just to shut them up. They left.

He thought, with a sinking feeling, that the prince had probably given in to a mad impulse under the influence of his fever and run away somewhere. The thought nearly drove him crazy. He ran to the river, looked over it, then came back and searched the empty mandapam. He shook out the hay bed he had made, went towards Uraiyur and came back again.

When he had done this about four times, he felt someone's presence in a tree nearby. He looked and then he realised that he was the second man at the waterfall in the forest. He crept towards the tree. The old man — it was Chitragupta — didn't know he had been found out until Ponnan pounced upon him and shook him fiercely.

"What do you want? Who are you? Why did you attack me?" cried the old man, astonished but regaining his composure quickly.

"You! Where is the king?"

"King? What king?"

Ponnan bit his lip and kicked himself mentally. "The man in the building, where is he?"

The man untied his upper cloth where it wound around his waist and showed it to Ponnan mockingly. "I had him right here a minute ago!" he said.

Ponnan was in no mood for banter. He raised a hand threatening to hit the man, who dodged neatly, ducked under Ponnan and disappeared. Then Ponnan heard a hooting sound, like an owl. He looked up a tree. The old man was sitting there, grinning down at him. "Ooooooo!" he said. "Fool! Did you really think you could harm a devotee of Mata Kali?"

Just like that, Ponnan had one of the most brilliant inspirations of his life. "I joined the Mother's followers long ago, old man," he said. "I have been foolish. What am I going to tell the Kapala Bhairavar when I see him?"

"Are you also one of us?" Chitragupta was surprised. "What orders were given you?"

"I was told to bring the one I would find in this mandapam to Kolli Hills. Now I have failed. He is nowhere to be found. Oh, what shall I tell the Bhairavar?' said Ponnan sadly.

"Why didn't you tell me earlier? A little while before you came, a procession stopped by. In it were the son and daughter of the Kanchi emperor. They stopped near this mandapam. They took a man from it, put him in a palanquin, and went away. I do not know who he is. Do you?"

Ponnan scarcely heard his question. He recalled that a huge procession had passed by when he was coming back with the physician and cartman. When he saw Kuntavi Devi on horseback, he had hidden from her. He had not thought to look inside the palanquin. But now he cursed himself. He realised the old man was telling the truth.

"Why are you silent? What are you thinking?" said the old man in the tree.

"What am I thinking? I am thinking how to sacrifice you to your precious Kali!" cried Ponnan, and threw a huge stone at his head. The old man puckered up his lips and made the same sound he had made at Vikraman when threatened. It stopped Ponnan dead in his tracks. Then he turned on his heels and ran like a man possessed towards the road to Uraiyur.

He must have run a kada until he reached a small village called Parantakapuram. There was more going on there than the usual hustle and bustle. Upon inquiry, he learned that the heir and daughter of the emperor were both in the village for the night.

Ponnan decided to find out what he could while they were there. With this in mind, he crouched behind a providentially located high fence and listened to the gossip of two serving girls who were apparently handmaidens of the princess. Their talk was mostly giggle and girlish chatter, but he managed to gather that Vikraman was in the camp, he was safe, the physician was taking care of him. The girls' opinion was that the princess was taking him with her so she could ask him about the king of Shenbaga Islands.

Ponnan had heard all he needed to. There was a fierce joy in his heart. He stood there a while, then turned and walked away into the night.

Ponnan's Thoughts

The royal party passed by Ponnan as he walked down a road in Purantakam. He felt a surge of respect as he saw Kuntavi's face. She was such a good woman! Why else would she have taken a sick man into her own palanquin? Ponnan wondered what to do next. Vikraman was safe with Kuntavi Devi right now. She was going where he wanted to go, and she would take him there. But he had to rescue Arulmozhi Devi. For that, he needed the help of the Shivanadiyar who had asked Ponnan to meet him at the old sculptor's house near Mamallapuram if he had any news. Ponnan decided to go there immediately.

He was aware of the danger Vikraman was likely to be in while in Kuntavi's care. What would happen if in a delirium he blurted out something that made Kuntavi suspicious? The penalty for defying the banishment order was death. What if Vikraman gave himself away accidentally?

That would not happen. If Kuntavi did find out, she would try to save him. Ponnan remembered that she had argued for his life three years ago.

Why did Kuntavi so badly want to capture the Shivanadiyar that she would launch such a manhunt for him? Who was the Shivanadiyar, anyway? When Vikraman had been rescued by the spymaster, he had been taken to a sculptor's house in a forest. Was that the place at which he and the Shivanadiyar had arranged to meet? What was the connection between the Shivanadiyar and the spymaster?

Ponnan believed the Shivanadiyar was a good man. He had saved him once, after all, from Marappa Bhupathi. Arulmozhi Devi, too, believed in him. But Ponnan had stumbled upon a tigerskin, a rudraksha necklace, false hair and beard in an old temple of Ayyanar. All things the Shivanadiyar wore, and proof the Shivanadiyar was not in fact who he claimed to be. Who was he then? Friend or foe? Should he believe in him or not? What had the Bhairavar told Marappan about him? Why would Kuntavi harbour such deep hatred for him? Valli had a theory as to his identity. She had said he was King Parthiban himself, but this Ponnan simply couldn't believe. Hadn't the king died in battle?

None of this made sense. One thing Ponnan was sure of, though. When he met the Shivanadiyar, the first thing he would ask was: "Who are you?" On receiving a satisfactory answer, he would part with his information. If not, he would simply walk away.

Ponnan walked along, thinking, thinking. As he was walking down the path to the meeting place, he heard a horse come up behind him and quickly hid himself. He caught a brief glimpse of the rider and guessed that was the spymaster. Ponnan followed him at a distance. He found that the horse had been tethered at the very house in which Ponnan was supposed to meet the Shivanadiyar. Before he could collect his thoughts, a man emerged from inside. Ponnan was astonished.

It was the Shivanadiyar, standing there to greet him with a big smile.

Ponnan and the Shivanadiyar

Though there was surprise and suspicion on Ponnan's face, the Shivanadiyar was already saying, "Ponna! You arrived at precisely the right time. I was just leaving for Uraiyur. If you had come a little later, you might have missed me." He seemed oblivious of the major dilemma his companion was in. Anyhow, when they had sat down, he said, "Ponna! Tell me quickly what news you have. Many things have happened that I think you need to know. Do you know anything about the queen?"

"Yes," said Ponnan, and proceeded to tell him about the search in the Kolli hills and the fierce-looking man, and his strange companion, and how he had seen them go down the path. The rest of the story he did not tell.

The Shivanadiyar made Ponnan repeat the description of the man many times. Ponnan finally asked, "Who is he? Do you know him?"

"What I know is that the queen is certainly alive somewhere in the hills. Several things are becoming clear to me now. You ask me who he is. He is the high priest of those who offer human sacrifices. I have tried for a long time to find him. We need to quickly find out a few things. But there is something more urgent which needs our attention. You may be surprised, Ponna, to learn that the prince has returned." And he looked keenly at Ponnan. He saw surprise and happiness on his face. "Don't you believe me?" he asked.

"Why did he risk so much to come back?" asked Ponnan.

"True! He is in danger. Something seems to have happened to him on the way to Uraiyur. That, at the moment, is top priority."

Not having to fake it this time, Ponnan asked, surprised, "How did you find out all this? By what authority can you say he is in danger?!"

"You've changed, Ponna. You even ask me what authority I have to tell you the truth! All right," he said, apparently coming to a decision. "I saw the prince and spoke to him. I was the one who sent him to Uraiyur."

"Why?" asked Ponnan.

"Why? Why? Because I wanted him to see his home again. Do you know when a man truly falls in love with his home? When he returns to it after many years of being away. He would greet even a desert with joy, and the Chola nation is the most beautiful I have seen. I wanted to make him stay here of his own will. That way I will be able to fulfil the oath that I gave King Parthiban on his deathbed. I did not expect this danger to befall him. Oh God, what shall I say if Arulmozhi asks me?"

"What danger is the prince in?" asked Ponnan. "How do you know of the danger?"

"You seem to be playing a question game today, Ponna! I don't know what happened. I only know something did, and that is enough for me. He went from here on that horse you see there. After two days, the horse came back. Alone. I don't know what happened to him. I must find out. Can you ride, Ponna?"

"Yes. But first, there are some little matters I want cleared up. I want to know who you are."

The Shivanadiyar grinned impishly. "Ahh!" he said.

"I saw you come down the road as the spymaster, now you are a holy man. Why do I get the feeling that neither is the real you? I must know who you are, right now. If you tell me the truth now . . . "

"What?"

"I will tell you something you need to know. If your answer is unsatisfactory, I will walk away."

The Shivanadiyar noted the resolve on Ponnan's face. "All right then, I'll tell you. But you must swear that you will not tell another soul about my identity."

"Very well."

"Good. Well, then!" said the Shivanadiyar and, like he once did before Parthiban, pulled off his beard and hair. Ponnan took one shocked look at his face, and fell flat at his feet. "You, my lord?" he gasped.

"Didn't Valli tell you? She guessed a while ago," said the Shivanadiyar calmly.

"She's a malicious one. She told the lie of her life when she said it was the king!" he exclaimed fiercely. "Just wait till I see her!"

The Shivanadiyar heard Ponnan out about the events of the past three days starting with his rescuing Vikraman and ending with Kuntavi's taking him away in the palanquin.

"Vikraman is safest where he is. Now we must find the queen," said the Shivanadiyar.

On the Island of Spring

For one whole week, Vikraman didn't know whether he was in heaven or hell. He wandered in dreams of fire and waves, and the same thread ran through all of them — his duty to the Cholas and the mysterious woman he had seen in Mamallapuram. He dreamed that she rescued him from perils, and yet she vanished when he tried to speak with her.

He dreamt in this fashion, joy and sorrow mixed, for quite a few days. When he awoke at last, he found that his mind was no longer clouded. His memory was returning slowly and he soon recollected everything up to the time Ponnan and he had spent the night in the mandapam. He looked at his surroundings. It looked so familiar. He soon realised why. He was in a room in the palace on the island of Vasanta Maaligai. He wondered how he'd got here, who had brought him, and, most of all, who else was here with him. Then he remembered Ponnan. Where was he?

He barely remembered his dreams and delusions, but one fact remained clear even now — the woman was real. A serving girl and a physician had come to see him. He had not seen either before. They gave him whatever treatment he needed and looked to his comforts. Ponnan didn't come. Neither did the woman.

A day passed. The next morning, Vikraman felt he could

not stay in bed any longer. He felt strong again. He walked around a little. He didn't feel tired. He left the room. Nobody stopped him. He went slowly towards the river. He was seeing the scene again after many years, and as he walked among the groves and gardens, he experienced as sense of peace and happiness within. He reached the shore after a long time and sat at the edge of the water.

As he watched the river flow by, he saw a face in the water. It was the face he had seen in his dreams, the face that had beheld him with compassion in Kanchi, and in Mamallapuram. He wondered if he would ever see her again and sighed.

At that very moment, Kuntavi appeared behind him. She leaned against a tree and stood watching his back.

"Is It Really You?"

Kuntavi stood beside the tree for a long time. Her patience was quite exhausted because Vikraman showed no sign of looking up. He stubbornly kept gazing at the waters flowing past. She finally picked up a pebble from the ground and flung it into the water at his feet. It plopped and splashed water on Vikraman. The effort paid off. Vikraman turned around and looked up at her. His eyes widened. He seemed about to say something, but didn't.

Kuntavi waited for a while. Then she went over to where he was and sat next to him. He gazed at her intently, and then looked away several times. Finally she got up and said, "Well, I'm going."

Vikraman started. He looked at her and asked, "Did you speak?"

"Yes, I did!" replied Kuntavi. "I am not mute!"

Vikraman continued to stare at her, his mouth open. "Why are you going?" he asked at last.

"Well, I didn't notice you were about to speak. So I didn't want to stay." Kuntavi sat down again next to Vikraman.

"I was afraid," said Vikraman softly.

"Then you ought not to travel alone!" said Kuntavi.

"I wasn't afraid of you. I was afraid this might be a delirious illusion. I didn't want to spoil it by speaking," said Vikraman.

"So, what do you think?' asked Kuntavi, smiling. 'Is this a dream or an illusion?"

"If you were to allow me, I would find out if you were real or not."

Vikraman stretched his hand out towards Kuntavi's cheek. She did not disappear, as she had in his dreams. Ever so softly, his palm touched her cheek. And then, unwilling to leave it, lingered there. Kuntavi took his hand in hers and laid it back on his lap. With a smile she asked, "So? Are your doubts resolved?"

"Oh, yes," he replied. "Two things have become clear to me."

"What things?" asked Kuntavi.

"One, you are real. Not a dream or illusion — real. And two, I cannot live without you any longer."

Kuntavi turned her face away from him and wiped the tears in her eyes. "So you remember me . . ." she said.

"If you had asked me if I remembered anything but you, the question would have been simpler to answer. Night and day, asleep or awake, in sorrow and joy, your face never left my mind. For three years, wherever I was, you were with me in my heart . . ."

"Three years? But it is only ten days since I met you on the street in Mamallapuram!" said Kuntavi slyly.

"It must be an after-effect of the fever. It seems like I've known you for years! Besides, if you keep looking at me with those dark eyes of yours, I forget everything. How should I remember days and months?" responded Vikraman.

"You are still feverish, I think," said Kuntavi. "That is why you are overflowing with grand words. You shouldn't have come here alone."

"I burn, but not from fever," replied Vikraman.

"All right then, look away from my eyes and tell me who you are and where you are from. If you can remember."

"I was sitting here doing that when you came. I am from Shenbaga Islands. I came by ship to trade in jewels . . ."

"You recall meeting me in Mamallapuram? Why didn't you come to the palace? Why did you leave for Uraiyur?"

"Shall I tell you the true reason?" asked Vikraman after a pause.

"If ever a merchant could tell the truth, tell me."

"I was afraid then that if I saw you again, I would never be able to leave you."

"Do they teach flattery as an art in the Islands?" said Kuntavi with a crooked smile.

"You forget. I was born here and I grew up here. I longed for these places all the years I was in the Islands. You saved my life. How can I thank you?" said Vikraman fervently.

"Why thank me? It is to the devi that you owe your life."

"To *whom*?"

"To the chakravarti's daughter, Princess Kuntavi. She was the one who gave us permission to bring you along. You owe her."

"Is that so? There are many things I need to know, it seems. But first, what is your name, and who are you?"

"My name is Rohini. I am the princess's companion." She forgot that she had introduced herself as Madhavi when they had last spoken to each other.

"Rohini. A beautiful name. I have seen Rohini shining beside the moon. But I don't believe she was half as bright as your eyes," said Vikraman.

"I've found you out now," said Kuntavi, teasing him. Vikraman stiffened. "You are not a merchant, you are a poet!"

"That is only because of your face, which shines like the moon in the dark summer sky."

"All right, stop your flattery. I have had enough of it."

"Flattery?" said Vikraman with a sigh. "If you don't like it, I won't. Tell me, how did I get here?"

She replied, "You were in a mandapam on the rajapattai. How did you get there? If you could tell me that, I will oblige you with what you want."

Vikraman told her all that had happened to him, taking care to conceal his identity.

Kuntavi heard him out silently and then said, "The chakravarti's son and daughter, Mahendran and Kuntavi, were journeying from Kanchi to Uraiyur. I was with them. I heard a voice calling out, 'Mother! Mother!' from inside the mandapam, and found you. The devi graciously consented to take you along and even agreed to let you stay here until you got better."

"In my delirium, I saw your face almost continually. It was true," said Vikraman wonderingly. "It was no dream, you really were there, weren't you?"

"I did visit you a lot while you were sick. You were saved because of Kuntavi Devi's generosity, you know," said Kuntavi.

Vikraman remained irritatingly silent. After a pause, Kuntavi said, "I have said so much about the princess, yet you have not a word of thanks for her!"

"I can never thank a Pallava!" replied Vikraman. "Where are the prince and princess now?"

"The crown prince has returned to Kanchi. There is some man from China who is visiting us. As the emperor is engaged in some other work, the prince has gone to Kanchi to receive him. Is it not a privilege for the Chola nation that it lives within the boundaries of such an empire? The prince of the realm actually refused to live under the emperor and — look at him now, wasting away in the Shenbaga Islands. Was he right? What do you think?" She looked at him eagerly.

He looked into her eyes and said, "As far as I can tell or know, it is far better to be a free man in the Islands than to be an enslaved Chola in a conquered country."

Each knew who the other was. Yet neither was willing to reveal this. How long would the charade continue?

The Secret Passage

The sun's first rays flattered the slope of the Kolli hills. The golden side of trees and rocks made a sharp contrast to the elegant shadow that stretched away. Birdsong filled the air and mingled pleasantly with the gurgling of a mountain river as it sped along its path.

A pair of stallions was coming towards the edge of the mountain. Seated on them were Ponnan and the Shivanadiyar, going upriver.

The Shivanadiyar gestured dramatically towards an unassuming boulder and said, "Ponna! What do you make of that?"

"What am I supposed to make of it? It's a bald rock, that's all."

"Look again. Don't you see the form of Nandi lying down, legs folded, head up?"

Ponnan looked and cried out, "It does look like a Nandi!"

"Ponna, you have just discovered the difference between a layman's eye and the sculptor's eye," said the Shivanadiyar. "When a sculptor sees stone, he sees also the form of an animal or being or god within it, hidden in its shape. He knows, you understand? He can see what lies beneath and how to bring it out."

Ponnan cut in. "Swami! Are you . . .?"

"Yes indeed, I am a sculptor! In this world, the thing I best love doing is sculpting. As soon as I finish this business, I am going to – Oh, never mind. Have you seen Mamallapuram?" he asked abruptly.

"Only once, yes," replied Ponnan, surprised.

"And what did you think of it?"

"It felt as if I were in a – a dream world."

"But they are real, those sculptures," said the Shivanadiyar. "As real as you or I, even more real. Long after you and I are gone, and our children's children, those 'lifeless' stone carvings shall enthral the world. A thousand years they shall live in this world. Once, Ponna, a long time ago, I dreamt of making all the land as I have made Mamallapuram."

"What! Did you have a dream too?"

"Yes. Did you think only your king could dream? He dreamt of the land of Cholas. I, however, dream of the whole Tamil land, of every race other than mine as well. Listen, Ponna! This Bharatam we live in, has been divided in two, the north and the south. In epic, song and learning, the north has always been famed. Only the kings of the north have been acclaimed. Chandragupta of Pataliputra, Ashoka Chakravarti, Vikramaditya! Even in our times, can you say that Mahendra Chakravarti is as famous as Harshavardhana? And do you know why the south is so far behind? It is because we have been split into Pandiya and Chola and Chera for as long as anyone remembers. Without one single large empire, no king or emperor can accomplish anything worthwhile. Harshavardhana's empire stretches across two hundred kadas. Here in the south, walk ten and you have crossed three kingdoms. Mahendra Varman dreamt of uniting the Tamil land into one, and he knew, as I do, that that was the only way the dream could come true. I had hoped I would live to see it come true. And then the dream was wrecked by one man's bravery."

"Who was that?" asked Ponnan.

"Why, your precious King Parthiban, of course! Ah, it was a war to remember, the war on the banks of the Vennar. It's still clear in my mind. The river ran red that night, and the moon shone silver and full upon the battle. And if there were fully ten thousand men there on the Chola side of whom none would return to tell the tale, imagine what a glorious battle it must have been." The Shivanadiyar spoke with feeling.

"Alas, I was not among them," said Ponnan sadly. "Such a death was not granted to me."

"It takes courage to die bravely, certainly," replied the older man. "But it takes greater strength not to fall into despair and go on, no matter what. You have that, so does Valli. You are luckier than you know."

"Tell me again about the battle on the Vennar," said Ponnan, and since the storyteller was unflagging and the listener was eager as far as that tale went, the Shivanadiyar obliged.

After a while, they came to the spot where the river narrowed and fell steeply from the mountains. The horses could go no further from there, so they left them in a thicket on the slope. When Ponnan asked whether they should be tied up, the Shivanadiyar replied, "These horses sometimes have more intelligence than the average human being. One of these brought tidings of Vikraman's danger before you did, after all. If I leave them here, they will stay here. If you tie them up, on the other hand, they may fall prey to wild beasts." He stroked them both gently on the back before they continued on foot up the slope.

The Shivanadiyar quickly made way over the rocks, small and big, that lay in their path, easily jumping from one to another, when required. Behind him, Ponnan gasped and panted and struggled.

"Is there something, anything, you can't do?" he asked finally.

"Oh yes, there is. I never could learn to break my word," came the reply.

Before Ponnan could understand the implications of the Shivanadiyar's statement, he went on, "The promise I made your king destroyed my dream, my very life."

"How could that be? You said so before as well, but I still don't understand," said Ponnan.

"Well, when I returned from Vatapi, I had dreams of making the south one great empire. I hoped to erase even the concept of a Chola or Chera or Pandiya nation, and instead create an empire, a Pallava empire. But Parthiban's courage ended my hopes. I promised him that I would make his son a brave man, a prince who desired nothing more than to be a free ruler of a free country. And then, all of a sudden, I found myself working for the welfare of the Chola kingdom! And now? Now I find myself cursing the night I set out to find Parthiban at his deathbed. I think this is what they call fate, no?"

The sun had reached its zenith and was blazing down upon the climbers when they heard the muffled roar of the waterfall. Ponnan informed the Shivanadiyar that there was no way further up. The Shivanadiyar nodded thoughtfully and began to study the surroundings.

One side of the waterfall was covered with thorn trees and creepers, and offered no way past. On the other were tall, sheer, smooth faces of rock, quite impossible to climb. The force of the waterfall had riven a deep pool into the ground. There was no way to get into the pool, except by following the path of the water. This was the path the Shivanadiyar began to test.

Holding on to the slippery rocks on either side with hands and feet and walking or sometimes swimming in the treacherous water, he moved steadily forward. Ponnan, watching, saw him finally disappear behind the waterfall. He waited eagerly, tensely, for some sign of the Shivanadiyar's return. He thought briefly of the consequences if the other man died. Ponnan's head began to swim. In the end, he decided to seek him out rather than sit there and wait. And Ponnan descended into the swirling waters.

Ponnan Departs

At that moment, the Shivanadiyar appeared on top of the mountain and waved to Ponnan to follow. The Shivanadiyar then led him to the gap between the wall and the waterfall. It was only a few feet wide, poorly lit, not to mention the prospect of an unpleasant death awaiting whoever slipped. They pressed ahead gingerly.

Then the Shivanadiyar indicated a small hole through which a man could pass, and started off up the path. Ponnan followed. They had to use both hands and feet, for the slope was steep. After they had gone some way in this fashion, there was a faint glimmer of light at the end of the tunnel. As it grew brighter, the form of the Shivanadiyar vanished into the light. Ponnan was right behind, and he had never been happier than he was then to step out into the light of day.

They stood, Ponnan realised, upon the very edge of the waterfall. The river screamed as it sailed out into nothingness to their left. Turning the other way, Ponnan's eyes widened in shock. Three mountains stretched around them, curving away from the vast base they grew from. The valley itself was covered with flowering plants, a glorious blaze of yellow.

The Shivanadiyar said, "The Kapala Bhairavar's hideout is

somewhere here or in the mountains above. I will go back only after I learn where it is. You must go to Uraiyur."

"What could be more important than finding the queen?" asked Ponnan indignantly.

"When we rescue her and she asks us, 'Where is my son?' we had better have a reply, I tell you. And besides, the prince himself is in great danger. If Marappan finds Vikraman is within his reach, who can say what he might do?"

"But how can I leave you alone? Especially now that I know why the Kapala Bhairavar wanted you for a sacrifice!"

"I have dealt with things like this all my life. I want to meet that Bhairava face-to-face, and alone. Might even clear up a few doubts I have."

"What doubts?" asked Ponnan.

"When the time comes, I shall tell you. Go to Uraiyur. If no danger threatens the prince, leave him on the island. Otherwise, bring him to the house near Mamallapuram. I will wait for you there."

"And if you do not come?"

"Wait until the next full moon, and if I am not at Mamallapuram or Uraiyur or the sculptor's house, you may look for me."

"As you wish, Swami," replied Ponnan. Standing at the edge of the pool, he looked up one last time. The Shivanadiyar raised a hand in blessing. Then Ponnan began walking quickly back down the slope.

Valli's News

Ponnan reached Uraiyur without mishap and went directly to meet Valli at his aunt's house. She was not her old carefree self any more. The members of the royal family she had loved and respected were all gone. Ponnan too had left. She had grown thin and frail, her happiness seeming to have drained away. When she saw Ponnan, her face brightened.

"Come in! Come!" she said, taking his hands in hers. "I was beginning to wonder whether you too had been banished, like the prince. Or whether someone had sacrificed you to Kali. What news do you have?"

"Good news and bad news and exciting news! But first, I am going to eat — I am starved! After so many days of eating whatever I could find, your kambu adai will be the food of gods."

"Eating whatever you found has put another inch around your waist! I worried, but now I wonder why I bothered. And I also have some information," said Valli.

"Okay, let me tell you quickly: the prince has returned to the mainland," said Ponnan.

"Really? Where is he now?" asked Valli eagerly.

"Wait, listen. The queen has been found, or at least we know her whereabouts. The Shivanadiyar went to rescue her. Valli, you are a cunning woman. You lied to me about the Shivanadiyar, didn't you?'

Valli acted the innocent and wanted to know about all that had transpired.

"Only if you'll stoke that stove," said Ponnan, and told her the whole story. When he finished, he asked for Valli's news.

"Oh, that? Marappa Bhupathi has been here five times in four days. He is now the Chola general and it has made him disgusting company. He kept on asking me about some jewel merchant who was on Vasanta Maaligai and whether he came from Shenbaga Islands. When I convinced him that I really didn't know, he kept coming and asking whether you had come back. He's already made one visit today."

Ponnan was lost in thought for a few seconds. Then he said, "There is no time to waste, Valli. I must get to Vasanta Maaligai. Is the boat safe inside our house?"

"Of course. But how will you get permission to go there?"

"Simple. I am under orders from the chakravarti that if Kuntavi Devi comes to Vasanta Maaligai, I am to ferry her wherever she wishes to go."

They concluded their meal quickly and went to the docks. The first thing they did was to get the boat out. Ponnan told Valli he would be back by nightfall and pushed off from the bank.

After so many days, the familiar feel of boat and oars on the Kaveri gave Ponnan a wonderful feeling. He guided the boat towards a lonely corner of the island. But when he looked up again at the island, he couldn't believe his eyes. For there was King Vikraman himself, standing there as large as life, one foot in the water and one on land, looking as surprised to see Ponnan as Ponnan himself. In two strokes, Ponnan had reached land.

The Boat Moves

The minute Ponnan got off the boat, Vikraman threw his arms around him. "If there is such a thing as a saviour, it would certainly have to be you. I've been looking at your house on the other side. If I hadn't seen your boat, I would have tried to swim across."

Ponnan quickly tied the boat to a root and they sat down to talk.

"Tell me what happened, Ponna! Everything, here and now, seems to me to be like a dream. When did you leave me, and why?"

"If you only knew how I felt when I left to fetch a physician and found you missing . . ."

"You went to fetch a physician? Why?"

"Do you remember falling asleep in the Mahendra Mandapam?"

"Yes, I remember it somewhat."

"We had wanted to go to Uraiyur the next morning. You collapsed and we couldn't leave the mandapam. I was half dead with worry and hunger. I couldn't leave you and I couldn't take care of you. In the end, I left to bring a physician. When I came back, you had vanished! I nearly went crazy!"

"After that?"

Ponnan told Vikraman of all the experiences he had had.

Ponnan's meeting with the Shivanadiyar surprised Vikraman. "That was where I met the spymaster!" he exclaimed. "And you met the Shivanadiyar in the same place. That could mean something else."

"What?"

"That the Shivanadiyar is the spymaster. But surely he won't give us away?"

"Never!" asserted Ponnan. "He made a promise to your father. But there is another danger. Marappa Bhupathi will be looking for you. We need to go from here."

"There is a greater danger here than Bhupathi, the danger of a woman's eyes," said Vikraman sadly. "Three years ago, when I was a prisoner of the emperor, I saw a woman on the streets of Kanchi. I saw her again on the docks at Mamallapuram. I spent three years on Shenbaga Islands and I never forgot her. She was the one who rescued me from death in the Mahendra Mandapam. I know men have been destroyed by love for a woman, but I never thought it would happen to me. That woman has me trapped, Ponna!"

Ponnan cut in. "Maharaja! I am no scholar, nor am I wise. But what of the men who were propelled to greatness by women? Rama and Sita, Krishna and Rukmini, and so many others!"

"You are right, Ponna. Even a Parthiban is made complete by an Arulmozhi, and a Ponnan by a Valli." Vikraman's voice went low. "Some men are made greater by their women. And gods who became lesser than men because of their women. It seems I am one such. My love for her is forcing me to abandon my duty, my ideals. I can't live without her. I would give up heaven for her. What price is the Chola nation or freedom? Enough to live with her, enough to pay taxes to Narasimha Pallavar."

Vikraman sighed at Ponnan's shocked look. "My resolve is growing fainter by the day. I have to leave right now. I'm ready to come with you immediately. Shall we go?"

"We shall, but we still have work on this island," said Ponnan. "Don't you remember? The box! I buried it on the island!"

"See? I forgot that too! Another two days of this and I will not know my own name!" said Vikraman.

After they had left, a shadowy figure moved from the concealing shelter of some trees. It loosened the knot that bound the boat. The boat drifted out and was soon lost to sight. As she watched it drift away, a sly smile spread across Kuntavi's face.

Buried Treasure

Ponnan walked into the mango grove, followed by Vikraman, and began searching among the trees until he found one tree with the figure of a tiger carved roughly into its trunk. He cleared the leaves beneath the tree and began to dig. When Vikraman made to join him, he stopped him, saying, "You are not yet well enough and you have many arduous tasks ahead of you."

Vikraman obeyed. He thought how ironic it was that he had stayed in his own home only by the grace of a foreign woman. But it will all be over today, thank God. Get the box, and leave! Not a minute more, not one more minute! He thought of his mad wish to see his homeland again, and now, when he had got there, all he wanted to do was leave. He felt a sudden hysterical desire to laugh. This was not the land his father had ruled. It was dead, its spirit broken under the heel of the Pallava empire. The sooner he shook its dust off him, the better. What fault was it of the land if the people had become bad, he reflected, and sighed. Was his father's dream going to remain a dream?

"Maharaja!" hissed a voice. Vikraman started and then saw Ponnan lifting out a long box wrapped in skin. Ponnan flung away the covering. Inside the box were the manuscript and the sword.

Vikraman picked up the sword reverently and said, "Ponna! I had bitter thoughts in my mind just now. I hated this land and felt it deserved to be crushed under the Pallavas. And now, when I see this sword, that delusion is gone. Once, long ago, this sword ruled the world. It crossed the seas in the hands of Karikal Valavan and Nedumudikkilli and established the Chola Empire. Why, the people of Shenbaga Islands are the descendants of the Cholas who emigrated in the time of Karikala Cholan. I am their heir, their blood flows in my veins, their sword is in my hand. What could they do that I cannot? The words of the Tirukkural that I was entrusted with along with this sword say, 'Effort will reap rewards.' I had forgotten that. There is something very wrong with this country, Ponna. The very wind brings sorrow with it. I will not stay here any longer. Come, let us go."

Ponnan had stopped covering up the hole, and was gazing up at Vikraman who seemed to grow in stature even as he watched. The radiance of his face was mesmerising.

Then they filled up the hole and went back to where they had left the boat. There they got the shock of their lives. "Where's the boat, Ponna?" asked Vikraman in horror.

"I'll try to find it," Ponnan replied, and ran down along the bank of the Kaveri.

Kuntavi Sets a Condition

Immediately after Ponnan left, Vikraman heard a rustling in the trees. He spun around to see Kuntavi emerge from her hiding place. They regarded each other silently for a few minutes.

"So this is the nature of the Cholas, it seems. To leave a house without informing the host."

Vikraman kept silent.

"I was listening to the whole conversation. I saw the buried treasure being taken out."

Silence.

"I know who you are," said Kuntavi.

"Then you know why I deceived you," said Vikraman. "I am an exile. My being here is enough to cost me my head."

"Are you afraid?" asked Kuntavi.

"I wish to keep myself alive, if I can. I still have a few things left that are easier done alive than dead. I have a promise to keep, a country to raise out of ashes. I'd like to do it with my head on my shoulders."

"Ah, but you died in the Mahendra Mandapam. The life you have now is the one I gave you."

Vikraman thought for a while. "What you say is true," he

admitted, “not in one way but in many. You’ve had my life in your hands since the day we first saw each other in Kanchi.”

“So why didn’t you tell me you were leaving?” asked Kuntavi, growing steadily angry.

“I was afraid you would not grant me leave, and if you did not, I would never be able to leave you again.”

“Do you have such a low opinion of me? That I would keep you from doing what is right? Well, all that is in the past. Now let’s sit and talk until Ponnan returns,” suggested Kuntavi.

“Did you untie the boat?” asked Vikraman with a flash of insight.

“Yes. I thought you deserved it, sneaking away as if you were afraid.”

“Grant me leave to go,” said Vikraman formally. “I also seek your help. I need a boat to cross this river, and a horse to get to Mamallapuram.”

“Granted, but on one condition. When the ship leaves Mamallapuram, you will take me with you.”

Vikraman held her hands. “Did I hear you right, Devi?” he asked in a voice choked with emotion. “You are ready to come away with an exile, to marry me? You, the only daughter of the Pallava emperor?”

Kuntavi never took her eyes off the river flowing serenely past them. “Such doubt!” she sniffed. “But then I forgot. You think that all women are fickle.”

“Never. But . . . your father . . . the emperor . . . will he agree?”

“My father will not refuse me anything,” she replied.

“Maharaja!” said a voice. Ponnan was standing behind them.

“Ponna! When did you get here?” asked Vikraman. “The devi told me she untied the boat.”

"I heard, Maharaja. But why do we have to go to all this bother? Were the devi to ask her father a favour, he would surely reinstate you . . ."

Kuntavi had risen to her feet and there was ice in her voice as she spoke. "What did you say, boatman? Ask my father a favour — beg him a favour! — to save your king's life? I made that mistake once. I will not make it again. If by the power of the sword in his hand, your king carves out an acre of land to be his kingdom, I shall be queen of that acre. Were he to only own a hut as his rightful property, by rowing people across rivers like you, I would live in that hut. I might ask a favour for myself, but not for him! It would be a slur on his honour and an insult to his worth. If he were caught and sentenced to death, I would only ask to marry him before he was killed!"

"It seems, Devi, that you will have to ask that boon of your father yet," responded Ponnan quietly. "There are soldiers coming, several of them, in boats."

All three of them turned to look where Ponnan was pointing. From the rough direction of Uraiyur came four boats filled with soldiers. They were heading straight for them.

By the Chakravarti's Orders

As the boats drew nearer, Vikraman suddenly came to life. "Ponna! Draw your sword!" he cried.

Ponnan ran to Vikraman. "Maharaja! Don't fight with Marappan's men," he pleaded.

In shock, Vikraman asked, "What's happened to you now? Have you lost all your courage?"

"No. My courage is quite intact. Please. Grant me this one favour."

"Very well. Devi, guard this box carefully for me."

Kuntavi might have heard him, or then again she might not. She was furious as she stood watching the boats.

Marappa Bhupathi, of course, was the first to step out of the boat. He folded his hands respectfully and said, "Lady, I beg forgiveness for not asking permission to land upon the island. I have come to fulfil the chakravarti's orders."

The Pallava princess was in a rage. "Which chakravarti? What orders?" she asked haughtily.

"Your brother Mahendran's orders. He has given me instructions to capture the spy and bring him to Kanchi unharmed. See for yourself." He handed her a warrant stamped with Mahendran's seal.

She glanced at it briefly and handed it back. "Who is this spy?" she asked contemptuously.

"The man who is standing here, Devi!"

"He is not a spy. You may leave. Now!"

"If he is not a spy, then who is he? Tell me that, I pray," he said mock-respectfully.

Kuntavi's eyes flashed. "Bhupathi! Have you no care who you are talking to? You forget yourself!"

"I do not forget myself. As if I don't remember this man! He was exiled by the Kanchi emperor. If he is not a spy, he is a traitor. I must do my duty, Devi!"

Kuntavi was trembling with anger now. "Senapati! This man is my guest. If he is harmed . . ." she said and stood in front of Vikraman.

Marappan hooted with laughter. "So, the prince hides behind a woman!"

Vikraman's face reddened with anger and shame. He stepped out in front of Kuntavi. "Let's go, Uncle," he said and climbed into a boat.

Marappan jerked a finger at Ponnan. "Boatman! You too get in the boat!"

"Can you tell me why he should come? Or show me the order for his arrest?' asked Kuntavi. She was furious.

Marappan looked away from her. "There is no such order, Devi," he muttered, looking down. "But he has harboured a criminal, a spy."

"Ponnan is under my protection. He is here to ferry me. You have no authority to arrest him. Be careful, lest you step above yourself!" she said.

Marappan gestured curtly to his men and said, "Let him go!" And the boats went back towards Uraiyur.

In the Middle of the Night

The minute the boats were out of sight, Kuntavi whirled around to face Ponnan. "Bring Valli here. Immediately. We have many things to do. We need to rescue that king of yours and get him to Mamallapuram. There will be a ship waiting for him there on the night of the new moon. When it leaves, he must be on it."

"I – I don't understand, Devi!" said Ponnan, astonished.

"When your king was delirious," explained Kuntavi, "he rambled a lot and I was able to piece together who he was, why he came, and some other things besides. One of them was that a ship from Shenbaga Islands would wait for him every new moon night. So we have to see that he is in Mamallapuram by that time. Else my father will surely pass sentence on him."

Ponnan left in the boat Kuntavi had ordered for him. His mind turned and tossed more than the river he crossed. The thought that Vikraman, who should have been the ruler of the Cholas, was spending the night in his own prison cell was painful. Nobody would help him. Everyone was ready to do the emperor's bidding. Then he reflected on his own position. In what way was it different? But could he trust the Shivanadiyar? There was no doubt that Kuntavi truly cared for Vikraman and wanted to save him. She had already saved him from death once.

After thinking things out all the way across, Ponnan reluctantly decided to do things her way. When he reached home, he found the door locked and barred. Valli opened the door only when she heard his voice. She told him why she had barred the door — the Kapala Bhairavar and Chitragupta had gone past their house. She had overheard them speak of a rendezvous at the Ayyanar temple later that night with Marappa Bhupathi. In fact, Chitragupta was still hiding thereabouts.

Ponnan and Valli went to the river's edge. Ponnan deliberately made a big noise getting the boat into the water. He wanted Chitragupta to note his departure. Within half an hour, he was back, after leaving Valli with Kuntavi at the island. This time, he ensured the boat made no sound at all, and pulled it aground some distance east of the docks. Ponnan hid in the shadows outside his house, waiting.

Soon, Marappa Bhupathi came along on horseback. Chitragupta followed after him, running and walking, and Ponnan after Chitragupta, to the temple.

The Bhairavar and Bhupathi

The temple was an eerie sight by day. By night, it was petrifying. A man, or was it a demon, holding a flaming torch stood beside the tall, threatening figure of the Kapala Bhairavar at the entrance to the temple. The firelight made the red sandalwood and vermilion on the Bhairavar's face appear as alive as dripping blood. He wore a garland of skulls. Frightened to death, Ponnan came as close as he dared to hear what they were saying. Just then, Chitragupta and Marappan emerged from the forest.

"Great lord!" said Marappan and prostrated before him.

"Senatipati! Have you fulfilled the Mother's wishes? Where is the sacrifice?" came the Bhairavar's harsh voice.

"The sacrifice is safe, great lord," replied Marappan.

"Where? Where is it? Do you dare disobey the commands of the Mother, Senatipati?"

"No! Never! Great lord, I would never disobey the Mother. The prince was caught this evening, and to bring him here immediately would create too many complications. The boatman is right here . . . !"

Ponnan was shocked. His stomach seemed to have suddenly taken up residence in his chest. But it returned to its usual place at Marappan's next words. "I was unable to capture him.

The chakravarti's daughter prevented me from doing so. The princess is also here, great lord! She is helping the prince, and we may have trouble from her. But I will complete the rest of your orders as well. I will have your sacrifice brought to you by the night of the new moon."

"Marappa! The Mother has great things in store for you. She blesses you with – never mind. When will you give me the sacrifice?"

"Before the rising of the new moon at the Mahendra Mandapam near Parantakam. I will expect your men to be there, waiting for me. If they ambush us, they will meet with minimal resistance. The men I choose will be selected for their lack of bravery."

"Very well. But beware! The Mother awaits blood on the night of the new moon."

"There is one more thing. The boatman Ponnan was missing for some weeks. I sent a man to keep an eye on him. He returned just yesterday with important news. Ponnan and the Shivanadiyar were seen on horseback riding up a certain part of Kolli hills."

The Bhairavar's face contorted with fury. His face, being fearsome even in repose, now assumed a terrible aspect. Ponnan felt a shriek building in his throat, tried to stop it, failed. Luckily, he was so afraid that not even a whimper escaped his mouth.

The three men left after that. Ponnan did not dare move until the torch was out of sight. The slender moon was rising in the east. His mind was fresh and alert. A plan to rescue Vikraman was slowly taking shape in his mind. Marappan's intentions were finally clear. Since sending Vikraman to Kanchi awarded him nothing, he was going to have men kidnap him and take him to be sacrificed. Ponnan would have to get Vikraman out of their clutches and to Mamallapuram immediately. He would need Kuntavi Devi's help for that.

Uraiyur Jail

Vikraman could have laughed at the irony. He was incarcerated in the jail of the country he was to have ruled! His dreams, and his father's, would end in a sweeping arc of the executioner's axe. Marappan would kill him with great relish. He would vanish without a trace in the memory of his own people.

The Shenbaga Islands were small, but he had been happy there, and free. Whatever wish he had had to free the Cholas was useless now; they had forgotten freedom. He was going to die without seeing his mother.

And Kuntavi! He could never forget what she had said. That if he were caught and sentenced to death, she would not beg for his life, but only to be wedded to him before he was killed. Oh, the regal air with which she had she declared this! He would have come from much farther than the Islands to earn the love of such a woman. He would even give up heaven for her, as he had told Ponnan. Her loveliness – no, not that, though it was a part of it – the beauty of her nature and her character had drawn him from Shenbaga Islands.

As the night of the new moon drew closer, Vikraman's weariness increased. If only he could somehow escape from the cell before the new moon! If only he could reach Mamallapuram! If only . . .

In the end, on the evening before the new moon, Marappa Bhupathi came to his cell. "Well, my dear merchant, orders have come from Kanchi," he said.

For one frightening moment, Vikraman thought he was going to be killed. Then Marappan said, "You are to be taken to Kanchi, unharmed. We will leave an hour after dark. Be ready."

Vikraman felt a surge of hope. There would be opportunities to escape on the way. He would perhaps die trying to, but it would be worth it. And even if he were to be taken to Kanchi without mishap, he would be able to defy the emperor and tell him that he would never pay taxes, nor would he suffer to live under Pallava dominance, or any other. Kuntavi would be there, as well, and she would be enough for him to gain the courage he needed. What more could he want?

The Night Before the New Moon

Later that night, the cell door opened. Marappan was standing there with some of his men. They bound Vikraman's hands tightly and took him outside where a covered bullock-cart awaited them. Vikraman was put into the cart, accompanied by a few guards. Others stood in front of and behind the cart. Then the whole lot of them set off.

"Who is this boy you're taking, my friends?" asked a cheery voice. "And where are you going with him?"

Vikraman started. It was the cartman. But the voice was Ponnan's. What was he doing here?

A soldier replied, "Don't poke your nose where it isn't wanted! Be quiet and drive the cart."

"I am not inquisitive, but the rest of the city is. Everyone wants to know who this boy is. Some say he is a spy from Shenbaga Islands, and say he pretended to be a jewel merchant, and that he duped Kuntavi Devi herself, and that the senatipati himself caught him. Is this man the spy?" he asked all in a rush.

"Presume, for conversation's sake, that he is the one," replied the other.

"Where are you taking him?" asked the cartman.

"Where else? What a silly question! To Kanchi, of course!"

"Dear me! So far? And will seven of you be sufficient? Suppose someone tries to free him on the way?" asked the cartman.

"Silence, you in the front!" rapped out the leader, and there was no more talk.

All too soon, they reached the banks of the Kaveri. Everyone got down from the cart except the driver. A boat was waiting for them. A man with a torch was also there. The cartman turned around his cart saying, "So, see you another time. Take the spy carefully to the emperor. Oh, by the way, there is a forest river nearby, be careful around there."

His face came in clear view as he said the last. Vikraman's shoulders slumped in dismay. It was not Ponnan. And yet . . . and yet, there was something about the eyes . . . and then he saw that it was really Ponnan, cleverly disguised, complete with a false moustache.

He had said something about the river. Was Vikraman to expect rescue at the river? He took some comfort in the thought. They walked until midnight after fording the Kaveri, when they rested in a mandapam. At dawn they set off again, flagging a passing cart to take them to Parantakam, and by the time they reached it, it was dusk. Vikraman knew they were going closer to the river. If the cartman had been Ponnan, help could be expected somewhere near here. He wondered who would come, and when.

Vikraman noticed with surprise that most of the people were still out after dark. Most of them were dressed in virulent shades of yellow and in each group of four or five was a man holding a torch. When he saw that most of them held long, curved knives, Vikraman became apprehensive.

He caught the words "Bhadrakali", "sacrifice" and

"Bhairavar" from the whsipers of the soldiers guarding him. It was only then that he realised that it was the night of the new moon. Was this a trap by Marappan to hand him over to the Kapalikas? He would put nothing past the man. He saw then that the people were shouting, a low, eerie, insane cry, "Om Kali! Jaya Kali!" over and over again. He shuddered. He saw that the Kapalikas were drawing closer. The men guarding him had disappeared, and the soldiers in the cart with him were also jumping out and running away. There were shouts of "Where is the sacrifice?"

As Vikraman had been bound to the cart, he was unable to get away. Just then came a voice, "Maharaja! Don't worry. I am here." Incredibly, Ponnan was in the cart with him, he was cutting free his bonds. Two horses were waiting for them. Ponnan jumped on one, and motioned for Vikraman to mount the other. "There's not a moment to lose!" he cried.

"What is This?"

Vikraman and Ponnan yelled at each other over the wind as they rode.

"Ponna! Were you the carter? The one with the moustache?"

"Yes, I was!" grinned Ponnan.

"I thought you had forgotten me!"

"The devi would never have let me!"

Vikraman's heart felt as if it was going to burst. "So where are we going?" he asked.

"Mamallapuram, where else? We'll reach in time to board the ship."

"Where is the devi? I would have liked to say goodbye to her one last time."

"The devi is in Mamallapuram, but she will not bid you goodbye."

"Ah!" said Vikraman. The heady night ride, the feeling of being free, and the knowledge that Kuntavi was in Mamallapuram, all gave him the feeling of being high up in the clouds. Then something struck him. "Why did you say I would not be able to say goodbye to her?" he asked Ponnan.

"The devi is insistent that you will not take her leave. She is going to accompany you."

Vikraman was silent for a long time after that. Then a sharp, "Maharaja!" from Ponnan brought him back to the world. He saw six or seven men lounging by the side of the road. Kapalikas!

"They were waiting here for you. Marappan's men were to hand you over to them. They won't be looking for two men on horseback. It'll be quite a while before they report to the Bhairavar and get their heads handed to them." Ponnan grinned gleefully. "The Bhairavar is going to have words with Marappan tonight."

"Ponna! I begin to think that you are the ancestral deity of the Chola clan! I don't know how I am going to bring myself to leave you, not knowing if we will ever meet again!"

"If you think I am going to stand by and let you sail off into the blue as I did earlier, you are mistaken. I am coming with you this time. Valli is already in Mamallapuram, with the devi. We are both going to be on the ship with you."

Vikraman was silent for a few minutes and then he said, "Ponna, if you and Valli accompany me, it would be as if the entire Chola nation were coming with me. But what of my mother?" His voice went very quiet. "I am going back without seeing her. There has to be someone here who can tell her of me."

Ponnan's mind was also struggling with the same thoughts. What had happened to the Shivanadiyar? Had he found the queen? He said, sounding outwardly convincing, "You need not worry about the queen. The Shivanadiyar is looking for her, and there is nothing he cannot do. He is not quite human, according to me."

"He asked us to meet him at the house near Mamallapuram, didn't he?"

"He won't be able to see us now," said Ponnan. "If we stop to see him, we'll miss the ship."

"True. Still, I regret leaving without seeing him or my mother."

Suddenly Ponnan exclaimed, "What is this?"

They were within sight of the river where Vikraman had nearly drowned. The Mahendra Mandapam was close by. There were two men standing with torches in their hands, along with some eight or ten other men, looking very businesslike and deadly. A palanquin lay by the side of the mandapam.

"A lot of fishy things going on tonight, it seems," muttered Ponnan to himself.

"Who would be here at this time, Ponna?" asked Vikraman.

"They might have been sent by Kuntavi Devi to help us," suggested Ponnan.

They drew up to the doorway, and halted. One of the men standing there appeared vaguely familiar to Ponnan. When he finally placed him, he was surprised. What were the men of Paranjyoti Adigal doing in the mandapam?

That man had also recognised Ponnan, and said, "Ponna! We found Arulmozhi Devi! She is inside here."

Mother and Son

Ponnan and Vikraman jumped off their horses at these words. And then a low voice, a woman's voice, came from within the building: "Kumarappa! Who is there? It sounds like Ponnan!"

That was as far as she got. With a cry of "Mother! Mother!" Vikraman had dashed past the startled Kumarappan. Arulmozhi Devi emerged from the mandapam. She was greatly changed. The woman who had been captured by the Bhairavar had been still youthful. Now, she looked as if she had aged thirty years in three.

Vikraman reached her in one step and fell at her feet. She slid to the floor beside him and took his head in her lap. Tears flowed down her face.

Ponnan had followed Vikraman inside. He looked around and the light of the torch revealed gnarled old Chitragupta, tied up. When Chitragupta saw Ponnan looking at him, he began to cackle. Vikraman heard the sound and he too saw him. He looked at Ponnan with surprise.

"Yes, this was the man who guided you from Mamallapuram," replied Ponnan.

Arulmozhi looked from one to another. "Will someone tell me what is happening? I feel lost. I don't know how long I was in that cave. I had just resolved to throw myself over the waterfall when the the Shivanadiyar stopped me, gave me courage. He told me Vikraman had returned, and if I escaped, I might see him again. Ponna, he told me you saved Vikraman from the river."

"Not only from the river, mother," said Vikraman proudly, "but from execution and sacrifice to Kali. He saved me more times than I can count!"

The old man cackled, "Sacrifice! There shall be a great sacrifice to Kali tonight!"

Three pairs of eyes stared at him. "Sacrifices galore! The Shivanadiyar will fall prey to Kali tonight! The reign of Kali is about to begin!" and again he laughed insanely.

Vikraman was on his feet. "Ponna, what is he babbling about? The Shivanadiyar . . ."

"Hee hee hee! He will be on the altar by now. And when midnight strikes, he shall lose his head!"

Arulmozhi looked at Vikraman and said, "He has been tormenting me with these words. The men who rescued me also caught *this* one —" she indicated Chitragupta — "while he was watching over me. Ever since we arrived, he has been saying that the Shivanadiyar will be sacrificed to Kali at midnight on the night of the new moon."

"What say you, Ponna?" asked Vikraman. "Of what use are we if we don't prevent this crime from happening."

"How can we do that? If we go to save him now, we won't reach Mamallapuram by midday."

"And if we don't? The ship will go away. That's all," said Vikraman.

Ponnan looked to Arulmozhi for help, saying, "Devi, he does not see the danger he is in. The emperor knows he has defied the exile order. If he is not able to get away tomorrow, he will certainly be caught by the emperor's men. If he goes to the Shivanadiyar, he will be in great danger. You tell him what to do."

Arulmozhi was bewildered.

"Mother! You are Parthiban's wife, and a brave woman. Tell me what I should do in this situation. Abandon the man who helped us in our need and run for my life? Do you think that my father would have wanted me to do this?" said Vikraman.

"If Vikraman is lost because of today's venture, how will he realise King Parthiban's dream?" chimed in Ponnan.

Arulmozhi looked at one, then the other. Her eyes stopped on Ponnan. "You may think me cold or unfeeling, Ponna, but to abandon a man who has aided us, protected us, been everything to us, merely to save his own life? I will not let my son do such a dishonourable thing."

"We don't know where the sacrifice will take place. Where are we to go?" asked Ponnan helplessly.

"Hee hee hee! I will guide you," said old Chitragupta.

They had little choice but to loosen his bonds. He began walking westward. Ponnan and Vikraman followed after him.

The Sacrificial Altar

They followed the river westwards for an hour and then cut north until they came to a lake. They could see smoke billowing in the sky on the opposite side. They saw some shadowy figures in the scrub. They could have been ghouls dancing among the ruins of the dead. The low drumming and the mournful crying sound of the instruments being played added to the eerie ambience. They cut across the bed of the lake. Even the horses trembled with fear. They pressed on for another fifteen minutes before they tied the horses to trees and went into the forest.

They saw some people dancing madly, as if possessed by spirits. Others were sharpening knives on the rocks; those clad in yellow were mostly meditating. Yet others were beating udukkais or small drums.

Suddenly, they came upon a clearing. On its right side was a bare hillock and upon it was drawn a huge image of Mother Kali in her most terrible aspect. Several figures were standing beneath the figure. Among them, and easily recognisable, was the tall, brown-haired Kapala Bhairavar, complete with his necklace of skulls, red sandalwood and blood-tinged vermilion on his forehead. He swayed on his feet as a demonic-looking man beat upon an udukkai.

A little further from him and to the front was a flat rock, a natural altar. Stretched out on it, bound hand and foot, was the Shivanadiyar. His expression was unafraid, despite his circumstances, and he was looking around to find some way of escape. A man stood by the altar. At the least gesture from the Bhairavar, he would slit the Shivanadiyar's throat.

Vikraman took in the scene. Then he sprang into action. He jumped out from behind the rock, and with one stroke knocked the knife out of the man's hand. It fell to the ground with a clatter. Vikraman stood by the Shivanadiyar and called out to Ponnan, "What are you standing there for? Come and help!"

The whole process, from Vikraman's leap to his call, had taken less than a second. The shocked, loud cries that rose from the devotees as they witnessed the sudden attack roused the Bhairavar. He walked unhurriedly to the altar and stood looking into Vikraman's face. And laughed.

He laughed loud and long, and the sound echoed in the suddenly silent clearing and rose beyond it into the forest. Every devotee, sensing that something was amiss, came running to the spot. As they crowded near the altar, the Kapala Bhairavar lifted one hand and roared out the single syllable, "Hoom!" Instantly, everyone was pushing backwards frantically. Even the man who had held the knife and was now looking at Vikraman murderously, stepped back quickly.

The Kapala Bhairavar looked carefully at Vikraman again and then said in a quiet voice, "Child! Are you not the son of the late King Parthiban of the Cholas? The Mother foretold that you would be here tonight. Truly, she is the greatest of all gods!"

His eyes, red and compelling, held Vikraman in their gaze. He was unable to look away. "Child, I came to Mamallapuram in search of you. That idiot Marappan interfered in my plans. However, I knew that you would be here tonight, despite everything."

Still enmeshed in his trap, Vikraman asked, almost whimpering, "Who are you? And why are you expecting me?"

"Tonight, the reign of Mother Kali shall begin in the fertile lands of the south. You are here to be crowned prince of the realm, and I am here to crown you. This is the command of the Mother!" Vikraman was transfixed.

Then, a single contemptuous laugh rose from among the watching devotees. It rang sharply in the deathly silence. Everybody, including the Bhairavar and Vikraman, turned towards the sound. It broke the half-trance Vikraman had been in and now he faced the Bhairavar boldly. "I understand nothing of what you are saying. If you are going to crown me prince of this reign of yours, then you would not obstruct me from doing what I must. The man here is a friend and benefactor of my family. He has helped my mother and myself greatly. It is my duty to free him. As long as there is a knife in my hand and breath in my body, I shall fight to free him." Knife in hand, Vikraman advanced towards the Shivanadiyar.

"Stop!" The cry that rose from the Bhairavar's throat was so forceful that it stopped Vikraman in his tracks. The knife he had touched to the ropes was frozen, still. The Kapala Bhairavar continued, "Vikrama, my child! This man is not a Shivanadiyar. He is an impostor, a fraud. And if you knew who he was, you would not be so eager to free him."

The genuine anger in the Bhairavar's voice bewildered Vikraman. He already knew that the Shivanadiyar was the Pallava kingdom's spymaster. So what? The other, sensing his advantage, pressed, "Ask this man who he is. If he has the courage, let him tell you!"

Vikraman stared at the Shivanadiyar and saw that he was smiling in pure joy. And then came a voice from somewhere, "Vikrama! First ask this man who wears the Kapala necklace as a disguise who he is! If he has the courage, let him answer!"

Every eye then turned to the man who had stepped out from the concealing shelter of a rock and was standing in the open. A gasp spread through the crowd as they saw his face. It was the former Pallava general, the bane of Vatapi, the siruthondar.

Nilakesi!

The sudden appearance of the siruthondar was the least of the surprises that sprang up in the next few seconds. From behind trees and rocks, even from within the crowd, fully armed Pallava warriors began revealing themselves.

The siruthondar walked towards the Bhairavar. His face was expressionless. But the Bhairavar had terror written all over his. As the siruthondar came near him, he trembled with fear. "You cheat! Tell these people who you are!" said the siruthondar. The Bhairavar fell down in a faint and there was a huge commotion among the frenzied worshippers. As they ran towards their fallen leader, the siruthondar leapt onto a rock and said, "My people! Devotees of Kali! If you want to know who this cheat is, come and I shall tell you."

Confused upon seeing their leader faint at the sight of the siruthondar, the devotees stopped to listen. "In a land which has fostered noble faiths like the Vaishnava and the Shaiva, the effluence of religions such as the Kapalika and Bhairava, which practice the filthy habit of human sacrifice, has been spread by certain people for some time. My friend — the prisoner on the altar — and I tried to find out where the root of this disease lay. In the end, he discovered the truth."

Someone called out, "Who is he?"

Others joined in with, "And where did he go?" The Shivanadiyar had slipped away unnoticed in the confusion.

The siruthondar continued, "You shall know in Uraiyur, two days from now. Now the truth of this man, this Kapala Bhairavar who lies shivering at my feet, will be known. Twenty years ago, in the time of the late Mahendra Chakravarti, Pulikesi of Vatapi marched upon the city of Kanchi. The atrocities Pulikesi's men perpetrated will not be easily forgotten. I led Narasimha Pallavar's troops to Vatapi. The chakravarti had ordered that no quarter be given. In defiance of his command, I let one man, and one man alone, walk away from the battle, for he had lost an arm in the fighting. That man became the Kapala Bhairavar. He is Nilakesi, Pulikesi's evil brother!"

A confused babble of sounds broke out as the implications of the siruthondar's words sank in. There were mostly cries of outrage. The siruthondar waited for the noise to subside and then said, "When the chakravarti learnt that I had granted him mercy, he said that what I had done was pure stupidity, that the consequences of my impulsive action would be serious. Which, as you can see, has been proved perfectly right. Nilakesi began spreading the foul ways of the Bhairava and Kapalika religions. He wanted to destroy by scheming what he could not conquer by might. He wanted to get you to rebel against the emperor. To this end, he concealed huge amounts of weaponry in the caves of the Kolli hills."

The Bhairavar had apparently woken up. An involuntary "Oh!" escaped his lips.

"That armoury has been raided, and the weapons given over to the army. This man also intended to trick the Chola prince

into becoming a figurehead for his scheming. To that purpose, he kidnapped the queen, Arulmozhi Devi . . ."

The Bhairavar had regained his senses somewhat and got to his feet unsteadily. "All lies!" he shouted. "What proof do you have for this? What witness can you find?"

Marappan stepped out of the trees. "I am the witness you want!" he said. "I will tell you the truth. This man, who styles himself the Maha Kapala Bhairavar, is no Kapalika. He is an impostor. He plotted against the emperor of Kanchi and asked me to join him. I refused. I have proof that he abducted, or attempted to abduct, the Chola prince on his way to Kanchi. I was sending him there on the orders of the emperor."

No one will ever know what thoughts ran through Marappan's mind in those final, devastating moments. Not a single person there expected what he did. With a cry of, "Let this traitor be sacrificed to the Kali he claimed to serve!" he ran towards the Bhairavar. Even if anyone had tried to stop him, they would have been much too late as he had already beheaded the Bhairavar in one wild swing of his sword. The next minute, Marappan had flung himself at the feet of the siruthondar. "If I have committed a wrong, punish me. It was done in anger. I know I should not have done this!" he exclaimed.

All those assembled there were still in a state of shock when suddenly Chitragupta appeared on the altar next to the siruthondar, and the knife he held in his hand swept sharply down upon Marappan's neck. Instantly, Marappan was dead. Soldiers rushed to restrain the old man who had now begun to cackle insanely.

Vikraman was revolted by all that had occurred. "Come, Ponna! Let us leave," he said. Only then did he notice that a silent ring of efficient-looking Pallava warriors had surrounded them. Their leader extended a scroll towards Vikraman. It bore the personal seal of Narasimha Varman and contained instructions to the effect that the Chola prince, who was being transported to Kanchi, should be intercepted and returned to Uraiyur where an inquiry would be held.

Vikraman quickly finished reading the letter. He glanced at his surroundings, and his hand dropped to his sword. "Maharaja, please don't be rash," said Ponnan. Something in his voice made Vikraman drop his hand.

The siruthondar had missed nothing and asked, "What message is this?" When he had read it, he looked at Vikraman and said, "Vikrama! Go to Uraiyur as instructed. I will come there as well, and bring the queen with me. When the emperor hears of what you did tonight, he will change his mind, I promise you. Don't be hasty and do something you may regret."

The next moment, the soldiers had marched Vikraman and Ponnan out of the clearing.

For quite a while after that, the siruthondar spoke to the people gathered there. He told them of the true nature of God, and about the brutality of human sacrifice. As a result, those who had come there to sacrifice or be sacrificed went home, much wiser and happier. But they were all wondering who the Shivanadiyar was.

The Sentence to be Passed

Kuntavi was waiting in Mamallapuram in a fever of anxiety. She kept going to the terrace and looking out. She had decided against going with Vikraman. It was too much of a betrayal of her father. No, she would send Vikraman on, find her father, explain to him. He would agree; she was sure of that. How many times had he said that he had made no arrangements for her marriage, that he would never presume to do that. She would have to trust her own judgement, he had said. He would not go back on his word now, she knew.

Then she wondered if she would have the willpower to take this course of action. Finally, in the afternoon, she heard horses stop at the gate. She had given orders that if a jewel merchant arrived he was to be brought to her immediately. But she received the shock of her life. The man who entered her chamber was her father!

"Father! Come in, come in! Where have you been all these days?" she asked in an unnatural flurry of words and action.

He smiled as he hurried across to stroke her hair. "Why are you trembling?" he asked, in a surprised voice.

"Nothing, Father! You came so suddenly," she said.

"Is that all? Sit down, child, sit down! When did you come

from Uraiyur? Why did you rush to see me so urgently?" he asked, sitting down. Kuntavi was more flustered than ever.

Thoughts were racing through her mind. If he came while her father was there . . .? Was there no way she could send Vikraman away without her father knowing?

The chakravarti noticed that she was disturbed and said, "I am going to Uraiyur this evening. There are several important things that have come to light. Arulmozhi Devi has been found by that false Shivanadiyar of yours."

"What! But who kidnapped her in the first place? Perhaps he was the one who . . ."

"No, no, my lady!' The emperor was very amused. "You still haven't dropped these suspicions of yours? The Shivanadiyar was not involved in the kidnapping. Quite the contrary. The leader of the Kapalikas, the Maha Kapala Bhairavar, was the culprit. The Shivanadiyar saved the queen from them. The reward was that he was captured and nearly sacrificed to Mother Kali. And guess who saved him from death?"

"Who?"

"The jewel merchant and that boatman Ponnan! And do you know who the jewel merchant really is? The prince of the Cholas, Vikraman. He had adopted this disguise to see his mother and his homeland once again. What courage, what daring!" The emperor sounded as if he was full of admiration for the prince.

"Father, where are they now?" said Kuntavi, her voice breaking.

"Who? Oh, Vikraman and Ponnan? They're in Uraiyur, of course! I ordered that they be sent there. I will conduct the inquiry myself. That is why I am going to Uraiyur. Do you want to come along?"

All the grief and fear that lay in Kuntavi chose to make their appearance at that moment. Flinging herself onto her father's lap, she buried her face in his shoulder and began sobbing loudly. A tear trembled at the corner of the chakravarti's eye, and he stroked his daughter's head as she cried her heart out. "If you want to tell me something, child," he said quietly, "you don't have to hide it. Why would you want to keep secrets from me?"

Little by little she told her father everything: how she had seen Vikraman bound in chains on a horse in Mamallapuram, that she was in love with him and wanted to marry him. Then Kuntavi began crying again. The chakravarti listened sympathetically.

"In this world, the only thing that stands supreme is love," said the chakravarti. "All else is ephemeral. When two souls unite in love, God himself as the embodiment of love stands witness to their union. To separate two people who are thus joined is a right that no one can lay claim to: not even a father or a mother. If you wish to marry the prince, I will not stop you. But there is one thing I must tell you. The Pallavas are known for never having failed to deliver justice. The chakravarti must live by the same laws that govern a peasant. If there are exceptions, there will soon be no law. The trial of the Chola prince will proceed like the trial of anyone else. He will be sentenced in the measure that his crime warrants. After the verdict is delivered, if you still wish to marry him, I will not stop you."

"What is the sentence for treason, father?" asked Kuntavi, although she knew what it was.

"Death," replied her father. "But in this case, there are other issues that I shall have to consider."

"Like what?"

"As you so have pointed out so often, he may not have been responsible for his actions. The false Shivanadiyar may have put him up to it. I shall have to look into the matter. The Shivanadiyar was also caught, and I will be questioning him as well."

Of course it's his fault, Kuntavi said to herself. If he had had the good sense not to get caught yesterday, why, Vikraman would have been safely on his way by now!

"And there is one other problem," the chakravarti said solemnly. "The problem of who gave the jewel merchant a horse and told him to go home quickly."

Kuntavi's eyes widened. "So what sentence shall you pass?"

"Let's find out. I shall award whatever penalty I see fit. Justice shall not be compromised in the Pallava kingdom," said the chakravarti.

An Order and its Execution

The inside of the palace looked like Indra's sabha. The chakravarti's chair was empty. On one side were his two children, on the other the Shivanadiyar and the siruthondar. Next to Mahendran and Kuntavi were Arulmozhi Devi and the siruthondar's wife. Behind them were Ponnan and Valli, very demure. In a chair directly opposite the chakravarti's throne, surrounded by Pallava warriors, including Achyuta Varman, was Vikraman, head held high. He was trying his best to look everywhere except at Kuntavi but every now and then his eyes would flicker towards her. Once, he caught her looking at him, and they dropped their eyes hastily, embarrassed.

Ministers and high-ranking soldiers, officials and priests, artists and poets and merchants and villagers from various areas had all taken their places.

There were others as well, seated tensely in a corner of the assembly. They were the men of Shenbaga Islands. It was not just the Chola prince who was on trial that day, it was also the king of Shenbaga Islands, and these men were waiting anxiously for the verdict that would seal their ruler's fate and, therefore, their own.

When the appointed time came and went and no chakravarti appeared, there was a low murmur of voices. The siruthondar rose and lifted a hand for silence. "People of this assembly! The chakravarti will arrive shortly. Until he arrives, I have been told to explain to you why this meeting is taking place."

"My friend, King Parthiban of the Cholas, died defending this country. His son, Vikraman, has been brought here for trial for defying his sentence of exile. His reasons for committing this crime shall be laid out before you here, and questioned. The chakravarti has decided that the people will be called upon to deliver the verdict. Before doing so, you will be given all the facts. Even though Vikraman disobeyed the emperor's order, someone has come forward to say that Vikraman has not acted entirely independently and admits that he was in part responsible for the crime." The siruthondar indicated the Shivanadiyar as he said this.

The siruthondar spoke of the time when, ten years ago, Parthiban had died protecting his country's right to be free. He spoke of the Shivanadiyar's conversation with the dying Parthiban. He then spoke of the events leading to Vikraman's exile, and those following his return, ending with the selfless rescue attempt by Vikraman as the Shivanadiyar was about to be killed. He concluded by saying, "People of this assembly, I wish to ask you only one thing. Has the Shivanadiyar fulfilled the promise he made to Parthiban — to make his son a freedom loving man, to make him brave and a fit ruler of a free country?"

When the cheers and cries of affirmation died down, the siruthondar raised his hand again and said, "I have left one thing out of this. When this man who sits behind me gave Parthiban his promise, Parthiban asked him only one question: 'Who are you?' In response, my friend pulled off his false hair and beard and showed Parthiban his true form. Seeing this, Parthiban died in peace, secure in the knowledge that his dream would be fulfilled."

There was a loud buzz as the people took in this information.

The siruthondar waited for silence, and then said, "I know you are all eager to know the identity of this man who posed as a Shivanadiyar. Well, then look!" and he spun around and whipped off the Shivanadiyar's wig and false beard. The radiant, serene face of Mamalla Narasimha Chakravarti was revealed.

The assembly erupted, there was utter pandemonium. Kuntavi rose from her seat and ran to hug the emperor screaming, "Father! Father!" in a totally undignified manner. Seeing that Arulmozhi Devi was about to faint, the siruthondar's wife held her and tried to revive her. Vikraman stared incredulously at the chakravarti. Not knowing what to do, Ponnan caught hold of Valli's hand and shook it furiously.

"Long live the chakravarti! Long live Mamalla Chakravarti! Jaya vijayi bhava! Jaya vijayi bhava!" There was a huge clamour and every single person in the assembly was on his or her feet, yelling whatever came to their lips. "Long live King Vikraman of the Cholas!" said Ponnan and the people enthusiastically took up this chant too, adding, "Jaya vijayi bhava!"

When the pandemonium had died down, the people realised that the Shivanadiyar was no longer in the room. The siruthondar then announced that Chakravarti Mamalla Pallavar would deliver his verdict on the matter of Prince Vikraman.

The chakravarti returned to the court, now dressed in the raiments of an emperor. The cry of "Jaya vijayi bhava!" rose up again as he took his seat. When things quietened down, the chakravarti said, "I have been given ample proof of your verdict on Vikraman. The penalty for defying the order for exile is death by beheading. I order that Vikraman carry the burden of the Chola nation upon his head — that is the beheading that I sentence. He and his descendants shall bear the brunt of ruling this land. As of today, the Chola nation is independent of the Pallava empire!"

The roar that rose now drowned everything that had come before.

A Dream Comes True

Vikraman was crowned king of the Cholas. Soon after, Kuntavi married him with great ceremony and splendour. As long as Vikraman and Kuntavi sat upon the throne, the Chola nation prospered. Trade flourished. The rains were abundant. Crops were good. Temples were established, the arts were protected and preserved, many new works were inspired. Goddesses of wealth and beauty walked along the banks of the Kaveri.

Still, Parthiban's dream remained a dream. As the planets are dimmed by the sun, the glory of Mamalla Narasimha Pallavar outshone Vikraman's fame. Even Vikraman's and Parthiban's brave deeds began to be credited to the chakravarti. The Pallavas carried their name and fame forward into many generations.

Meanwhile, the Cholas were bound by their narrow confines. But the dream was never forgotten. The story of Parthiban's life and death was kept alive by Vikraman and his descendants, and they took their sons to see the pictures he had drawn upon the walls of the Chitthira Mandapam, just as their fathers had done.

It was only some three hundred years later, when Rajaraja Cholan and after him, his son Rajendra Chola, ascended the throne, that the Pallava glory began to end. The Cholas conquered the north almost all the way up to the Ganga, the south up to Lanka, and several islands on the west and east, going all the way to what is today the Philippines. Ships bearing the Tiger flag, emblem of the Cholas, sailed far and wide, and the Chola flag flew all over the southern continent and its oceans. Magnificent temples and towers rose up into the sky, marking the fame and power of the Cholas. These examples of architecture still remain indelible symbols of the splendour of the Cholas.

And so, three hundred years after his death, Parthiban's dream came true.

AFTERWORD

KANCHIPURAM
CHENNAI
PALLAVAN TRANSPORT
MAHABALIPURAM
CHERAN EXPRESS
COIMBATORE
CHOLAN TRANSPORT
PANDIYAN EXPRESS
TIRUCHIRAPALLI
MADURAI

Mamallapuram and the Cholas

It was awkward to translate a novel without having seen the places I was talking about. It got worse and worse as I realised that what I knew of South Indian history could be written on a matchstick. I was never too fond of history textbooks. To me, history is the interweaving of individuals, events, attitudes and cultures, and their results, and there is precious little of that in those books. But Mamallapuram was something of a special case. After all, I knew a lot more about it than about most of the other places I'd written about, and I had a personal interest in it. So I went there, for the first time, a year and a month after I finished the translation.

Around two thousand years ago, South India was divided into four principal kingdoms. The South, at that time, included land south of the Tungabhadra, Sri Lanka and the various island chains around India. The four dynasties were the Cholas, the Cheras, the Pandiyas, and the Pallavas. No dynasty was dominant for too long — power and resources were spread too evenly. The fragmentation of these kingdoms had already begun before the British Raj. But they were revived in the bus systems! The Government of Tamil Nadu separates its bus services under the dynasty names. So if you were travelling in Tiruchirapalli, you'd take Cholan buses, Pallavan in Kanchipuram (and Chennai), Pandiyan in Madurai, and Cheran in Coimbatore. So that is an easy way to remember the capitals of these four kingdoms. (The Chola capital was shifted to Thanjavur before Rajaraja Cholan.)

The Pallavas were the youngest dynasty to rise — they held the northernmost section of the South. Their capital was Kanchipuram or Kanchi. The Pallavas, the smallest of the four, were the dominant dynasty for quite a while, and it was during this period of prominence that the major sea-trade base shifted from Nagapattinam, which was in Chola territory, to an island called Kadalmallai. It was later renamed Mamallapuram by Mahendra Varman after his son Narasimha Varman, who was accorded the title Mahamallan or Mamallan, meaning 'greatest of wrestlers'. Narasimha Varman was believed to have been a proficient wrestler.

The sea has always determined Mamallapuram's destiny, as a port and as a cultural centre. Its influence has not always been beneficial. The rising sea, my tour guide told me, is said to have swallowed six of the seven shore temples in a straight line out to sea. I could believe this. Even though I was a good fifty feet from the shoreline, blocked by a solid twenty foot wall of rock, I could taste the spray on my lips, and the sea hissed and roared up the beach to my side in all its destructive glory. The sea breaches the wall several times a year during the monsoons. Because of this, the sculptures of the shore temple have almost lost their identity, scraped and soaked and dissolved by the force of the sea and the chemicals in its water. The 'kundrugal' (small rocks with temples carved into them) that are found at regular intervals throughout the beach have suffered the same fate.

The history of Mamallapuram began when Mahendravarman the First conceived of an ambitious plan — to carve temples into and out of the huge monoliths that lay all over Mamallapuram. He brought the finest carvers from all over his dominion and employed them in the project. The descendants of the carvers continued the profession. Today, sculpting and carving and their associated arts are a major source of employment here, and a group of carvers, the Maayans, trace their origins back to the golden era of the Pallavas. There are several minor carvings on the rocks along Mamallapuram that are said to have been carved by apprentices — mostly the carvers' children. These are mostly carvings of animals — there was one monkey with a slightly 'duh' expression I liked.

I was extremely impressed by the mechanical expertise displayed by the ancient South Indians. Apparently, these Pallavas were real engineering whizkids. Keep in mind that they had virtually no machinery nor advanced measuring or surveying techniques, and listen to this: the hilltop temple of Durga at Mamallapuram is the exact same height as the temple in Tirukazhugukundram, some one hundred and eighty kilometres away. They are also precisely level in altitude! Another thing: there was a safe underground passage for the Pallava Queen Mother to go from her apartments to the Shore Temple and the other temple in the town proper in time of war. The real clinch was that all the entrances were at exactly the same level, and they were nearly a kilometre away! I had to keep reminding myself that all this was not done with modern technology, and appreciate it from a historical viewpoint instead of a contemporary one. The old jetty near the Shore Temple was just a few feet wide. So the ships that Kalki talked about couldn't have been more than six feet wide. That meant the ship must have been only, like, twenty feet long! And they sailed up to Indonesia and Arabia and Greece on that? What guts!

The most famous of the inland carvings is a huge bas-relief carving on a large cleft rock called Arjuna's Penance or Bhagiratha's Penance. The legend of Ganga's descent is imaginatively portrayed in this relief. It is several metres high, and has many subplots and associations. There are gods and demons, elephants, lions and men, and even a cat that is trying to catch a mouse (a forerunner of Tom and Jerry, perhaps?) by pretending to meditate in the same pose as Bhagiratha. The legend behind this carving is that it was done by a master artisan during a severe drought — he embodied his prayer for water in stone.

Other famous carvings are scattered over all the rocks of Mamallapuram, but my personal favourites are the five rathas. The step-like structure of the towers ensured that by standing at a certain height each layer was clearly visible. These rathas would be extraordinary by themselves, but picture this: they are monoliths, carved out of one stone. That means no second chances, no accidents, because an error couldn't be cut away while preserving proportions. Of course, only the best artisans worked on them, so I suppose that wouldn't have been a problem. There are two huge animals in the middle of the temples: a lion and an elephant. These are attributed to the symbols of two rival groups of artisans who carved different parts of the rathas. Even with so many people working on the rock, it took forty-two years for all the rathas to come to life. (Rocks need to have life in them to come to life under the artisan's 'uli', or chisel, says the guide — poetic, isn't it?)

Contrary to popular belief, these rathas have little to do with the five Pandavas. They are meant to convey the unity of religions. Although Islam and Christianity had not made much inroads into India yet, Buddhist, Jain, and even Greek and Roman gods appear in the rathas. At the time, the Vaishnava, Sakta and Shaiva sects were so different that they were almost different religions, and so they too have separate levels and temples. The Egyptian sun god Ra, his Greek counterpart Apollo, and the Hindu Surya share one level of a temple. There are carvings of people with Greek and Egyptian hairstyles and faces.

Narasimha Varman occupies a large panel on the back of one of the rathas, facing away from the entrance, on the opposite side of the Egyptian (possibly a trader) with the intricate hairdo. Like any passionate tourist who finds a local celebrity and has a camera handy, I clicked a couple of snaps of myself with him. He didn't seem to mind.

My trip to Mamallapuram was an eye-opener to South Indian history. It also spoke eloquently of a very great man and king — Narasimha Varman. As I stood on the shores of Mamallapuram I thought of him. If the legacy he left behind is so intriguing, how would he have been? Sometimes it seems nice if history could replay itself, so we could find out.

A final word. The monuments of Mamallapuram are being destroyed by unthinking tourists. This is a worldwide issue. Everywhere, scenic areas, natural parks and ancient structures are losing their unique qualities due to misdemeanours by visitors. Places like Mamallapuram are a part of the history of India and of the world. Every person who leaves such monuments untouched contributes towards preserving them for future generations. Let us do what we can to maintain our heritage.